# Their Amish Life

Alice Evans

Published by Trellis Publishing, 2021.

This is a work of fiction. Similarities to real people, places, or events are entirely coincidental.

THEIR AMISH LIFE

**First edition. July 3, 2021.**

Copyright © 2021 Alice Evans.

ISBN: 979-8224829491

Written by Alice Evans.

# THEIR AMISH LIFE

## ALICE EVANS

<u>Prologue:</u>

The tears begin to pool at Laura's feet as she rests her head in her hands. Propped up against the window frame, she begged for the pain to stop as she watched the world around her turn. They couldn't see. They wouldn't care enough to try. As the day drug on, one more piece of her shattered existence faded away as their smiles and laughter filled the outreaches of her mind. As their days rolled on, all of the things she had so desperately pushed down into the back of her mind had begun to rip her soul to shreds. Nothing in her life had ever been easy, but she never once complained; that wasn't who she was. Laura Miller stood in the face of adversity and simply stated that God had a plan for her and if this adversary is what He intended for her, she was willing to stand her ground with Him by her side.

For the first time in thirty-five years of living, however, she couldn't. For the first time, she couldn't hold onto the singular force in her life. Because if she aligns herself with Him, then she must also agree to the terms that the same person who is on her side is the same person on... *his*. After giving him ten years... ten years of devotion, love, and care, she must remain silent. Her cries muffled, her pain ignored. Then all at once, the pain becomes too much and as she clutches her chest, Laura falls to her knees; knocking into the bookcase.

As the Good Book falls beside her, her vision clears just long enough to read one verse; Isaiah 64:8. *"Yet you, LORD, are our father. We are the clay, you are the potter; we are all the work of your hand."* Whether fate, need, or celestial intervention, Laura dries her face and uses the limits of her strength to rise to her feet. She knows that whatever she chooses to do next, it will change everything. There is nothing she can do, but she can no longer sit around in passive silence. She must confront her fear and remain unshaken in her faith... but as she turns, her mind flings back once more to before this all began.

*"how did I end up here..."*

<u>Chapter One</u>

You are one in a million; there never has been or will there ever be someone who is exactly like you. Laura Miller heard this phrase uttered by every mother after she helped them to deliver their child. Hearing those few words always sparked a great warmth that would wash over her and spread throughout the home being created. This thought, of course, was always followed by a murmured chuckle as Laura realized how juvenile she was being. Despite these thoughts entering her mind, she had decided many years previous that she could not be happy without her job as a midwife. From the newborn coos to the mother's tears the moment she gets to hold her child for the first time, Laura found that nothing else in this Earth bound life could ever bring her the same joy.

For this, she considered herself very lucky. Some people are not as fortunate as she was in finding that her work and her passion in life were aligned completely. Whether due to financial constraints, personal inability, or and other number of factors, not everyone is afforded the same luxuries she praised God for everyday. As she packed up her kit to go into town, the hired hand her husband had hired to help fix the roof knocked on the door jam before entering.

"Ms. Miller, there's someone here to see you, ma'am."

"Thank you, Jeremiah, you can send them in." Jeremiah nodded his head and moved aside for a woman to enter her home.

"Thank you, ma'am for welcoming me into your home. I am sure you are quite busy so I won't take up much of your time-"

"Slow down, child. My schedule should not concern you. Besides, unless the Lord has any plans for Susan Price's child to be born two months early, my schedule is all but cleared for the day." The small woman stood in front of her, and though she smiled, her body language betrayed her true feelings. Short in stature, and thin in frame, if her cheeks hadn't been so flushed, Laura would have been convinced that she was sickly or malnourished. Scanning over the woman's stance and overall demeanor, Laura could tell that something wasn't quite right with the picture she was seeing.

"Would you care to sit?" Laura floated her hand to usher the woman into her kitchen. It took the woman a minute to collect herself as she situated herself in Laura's grandfather's handmade chairs. "What's your name, dear?"

"Sarah. Sarah Fisher."

"Oh, you are Ihrm and Mary Fisher's daughter right?" Sarah nodded her head briskly. "I don't think I've ever had the pleasure of meeting you. Though, somehow I feel like you already know me."

"Please don't think me intrusive. Susan is a friend of mine and she told me that you were the best person in town to speak to about... well really anything." At this point, Sarah's words flew from her lips. As if she had been bottling up her words for far too long.

"Susan speaks too highly of me. Maybe you would be better speaking to Preacher King. He lives just up the road if you would like me to escort-"

"NO!" The strength and anguish in her voice startled Laura; and frankly would have sent her reeling if she had been standing. Noticing the confusion her exaltation had invoked, Sarah quickly searched to find the words to save face. "What... What I mean to say is.... Well..."

"You want to talk to a woman, not a man is what I am gathering. Is that right?" Sarah nods her head vigorously.

"It's not that I feel shameful or like I am doing something wrong that the preacher can help me with.... I feel I just needed to talk to someone like you; especially after hearing about how helpful you have been for Susan throughout her pregnancy." Laura watched as Sarah's hand left her lap and began cradling her stomach. Though it had gone unnoticed before, Laura could now see a distinguishable outline.

"Sarah, are you pregnant?"

"Yes. Or at least, I think I am. My husband says we are so lucky to be blessed so soon after our wedding, and I agree..."

"But?"

"But... I wish I had been given more time to prepare for this. What if I mess something up and end up hurting my child?"

"The fact that that is your biggest concern proves to me that you will do nothing of the sort. Believe me, I have sat with many an expectant mother and they all share the same fears brewing in your mind. You fear that the love you have won't be enough; you worry that your husband won't care for you the same after the baby comes; you fear that you will somehow mislead the child and that he won't follow in our ways; I have heard every fear and worry in the book."

"And what do you tell them?"

"I tell them that it is all going to be alright. The Lord does not give His people something that they cannot handle; but that doesn't mean that it is sinful or shameful to ask for help. We all have good and bad days, but being honest about that makes it easier to make it to the other side." Sarah's face began to brighten as Laura's words of encouragement and love began to sink in.

"Thank you, Miss."

"You may call me Laura if you like." Sarah's smile then widened to encapture her whole face and the color had begun to return to her skin.

"Thank you Laura."

Chapter Two

"That's Mrs. Miller to you, girl." A gruff voice filled the house as Laura gripped the cloth in her skirt.

"Ephraim, please."

"I'd keep my mouth shut if I were you, Laura." Laura pushed her energy into her feet to stand, but she couldn't make herself move.

"I'm not sure who you are and I will apologize if I frightened you. However, I need to speak with my *wife* and I am going to ask you only once to leave my house." Sarah's eyes darted between the scene unfolding before her eyes. She nodded her head once before quickly exiting. Laura wished to have the courage to express herself before

Sarah's shadow escaped the stoop, but her eyes blazed with fear as her husband walked over to her.

A statuesque man, Laura always considered herself to be quick lucky to "land him." Before her father died, he insisted that he see Laura be married to a God-fearing, stand-up man who could take care of her. From the moment they were introduced, Laura was inexplicably smitten. From his dark auburn hair to his piercing green eyes with the little blue flecks, not only was he a man of God, but he was the kind of man she always imagined herself with. Less than three months after their courtship began they were married. The wedding was a large affair, larger than any other the town had experienced and they were gilded with praise and admiration for being the most successful match the community had ever seen.

But what happened behind closed doors was different. The first few months, even years were fine. They were happy and nothing seemed remiss. But as they approached their fifth wedding anniversary, something in him changed. As much love and support that Laura would afford her husband, he stopped smiling. The person the town saw during the day was not the man she would come home to at night. The man she knew and believed to be kind, open and charitable turned mean-spirited, harsh and oftentimes rude. Laura, despite all of this, gave him the benefit of the doubt. Maybe the business isn't doing well, maybe he isn't feeling good; perhaps he's just having a bad day... all these things and more ran through her head as she created excuse after excuse for his differing behavior towards her and others. This continued for another five years and unbeknownst to her, their tenth anniversary was about to pass them by.

Laura's inner monologue of running through the changes in her husband's behavior became readily apparent to him as he threw his hat down.

"What are you thinking about? What?"

"Ephriam, are you alright?"

"What, you work as a midwife and you fancy yourself a doctor?"

"That's not what I meant," Laura's mood began to fall as her husband's harsh expression fell on her heart. "I'm just worried about you. I am your wife, you should be able to confide in me about everything, and if something is going on that I need to know about-"

"Why would I talk about anything of any importance with you when you are never around?"

"I don't understand..."

"What, you have time for every terrified girl bringing new life into this world, but you can't afford me anytime at all?"

"When have I ever prioritized my work over my love for you?"

"When haven't you?"

"Ephraim, please, you aren't making any sense. What do you want from me?"

"Why? Am I scaring you?" Laura, now stood across the room, had laced her fingers around the locket encircling her neck. Her eyes unable to flutter from his. As piercing and afraid his expression made her, she could never seem to remove her gaze. As much and as often he confused her and conjured up fear in her heart, her love for him was unyielding.

"What, you can't find the words?"

"I don't know what you want me to say. I have sat beside you day after day as you changed before my eyes. My love for you has never faltered and even now with these accusations all I ask is that you are honest with me about what you want. Something has been bothering you for so long, but you won't talk to me." Laura could feel her own voice increasing in intensity. "Just tell me what you want! I can't read your mind!" Angry tears flow down her cheeks as she can no longer hide how unhappy she had become.

Ephraim felt every tear as if it were his own as they rained down his wife's cheeks. He knew what he was doing hurt her, but something in him was telling him that it was for the best. The hurt she felt now is what she deserved for taking him for granted all of these years.

"You want to know what I want?" Laura's eyes close as more tears stream down her face and shakes her head; as if begging him to reveal his pain to her. As he stares at her, looking for any shred of sincerity, he states his desires through the use of one word.

"Quit." And with that, Laura's heart broke.

<u>Chapter Three</u>

They didn't speak the rest of the night. Laura's heart hung heavy in her chest as she laid herself to bed that night. She didn't realize how unhappy her work had made him. But as these thoughts plague her mind, she feels Ephraim lay down beside her. Every bone in her body wants to roll over and wrap her arms around him; to provide him some sort of comfort that he can't seem to find within himself. As she shifts her weight in the bed, she feels him turn away from her, as if knowing the desires in her heart. Muffling her tears, she closed her eyes and drifted off.

Laura often found solace in her dreams, believing that God would often speak to her through her dreams and help to guide her towards finding the answers she needed. She prayed before finally drifting off to sleep for Him to give her a sign or to help her understand her husband's sudden fury with her desire to continue working. Tonight, however, it was not an abstract, objective vision but a walk through her own memories. She flies through her inner timeline until everything stops and she lands in a memory from so many years ago she had nearly forgotten about it's passing...

*"Are you enjoying yourself, Laura?"* Laura watches on as her younger self walked through the meadow with the younger version of the man she loved inquired of her feelings.

*"This is lovely Ephraim. How did you manage to find this place?"*

*"Well while everyone else went out on Rumspringa I stayed behind to help my father and mother in their shop. They are going to hand it over to*

*me one day, you know and I thought then was as good a time as any to get started learning the business."*

*"I'm sure they greatly appreciated that. But didn't you ever regret not getting to go out and experience the world before beginning your life?"* Laura, watching on, did not take that much stock into his responses or expressions that day, but she now finds herself unable to look anywhere else. She hid behind the seemingly singular tree in the vast valley she found herself remembering; though she chastised herself for hiding because as this is just a memory why should she be hidden? She, after all, was the one who needed to figure out why God was showing this to her.

*"Why would I leave when I have everything I could possibly need right here? Besides, now that you are back, why would I ever need to leave?"* Both Laura's blush uncontrollably.

"Ephraim, please."

"What? Do you know how distressed I was when you left?"

"We had never met before our fathers introduced a few months ago."

"No, but I saw you when you left town that day."

"You did?"

"As I saw you with your suitcase in tow begin to walk away from town, I ran up to the roof of my parent's shop to get a better look at you. From the instant I laid eyes on you I thought you were the most beautiful girl I had ever seen."

"Ephraim-"

"I didn't know how long you were going to be gone, but I knew that I would wait as long as it took for you to return."

"But you didn't know me. I could have been deranged or incompatible... what made you do a silly thing like that?" Ephraim stopped in his tracks, turning back to face her. Plucking a bright yellow field from her feet, he places it behind her ear; caressing her face as his hand falls to lock with hers.

"Something in me just knew. Whether that was God or my heart, I believe that He wanted me to know to wait for you to return. I mean I didn't think it would take four years, but better late than never I guess." Laura lightly wacks Ephraim with her free hand as he pulls her with him, running through the meadow.

Laura awoke as she felt herself intertwine with her past self as she was pulled into the meadow by the man snoring loudly beside her. Rubbing the vision from her eyes, the room was pitch black. She had no new answers, just further confusion.

"Why that memory?" She pondered aloud.

"Go back to sleep, Laura."

"Ephraim! I'm sorry, did I wake you?"

"Just because I'm angry doesn't mean I am not still concerned when my wife wakes up in the middle of the night for no discernable reason." Laura feels a smile and a small spark light in her chest. "Go to sleep, Laura."

She reaches to place a hand on her husband's shoulder, but finds herself holding herself back. She found herself at a disadvantage to her husband. Though she had never questioned his love for her, she never knew the depth of his love for her. That memory from so long ago that was tossed aside because of a frivolous girl's temperament now broke this woman's heart. A man who loved her so much to wait for her to return to their world couldn't answer for why she stayed away for so long. As much as she wanted to, everything they had built together would be destroyed if she did. Letting loose a sigh, her head falls back towards her pillow and she closes her eyes trying to escape the guilt boiling in her gut.

<u>Chapter Four</u>

When she woke up in the morning, Ephraim was nowhere to be found. She ventured around the house and both the front and the back yard before re-entering the kitchen. As she runs her fingers absentmindedly over the splits in the wooden table, she yelped as her fingers brush a piece of paper, slicing her fingers. As she tended to her fingers, she looked down to find a crumpled piece of paper lying on the table. Laura felt a stone lodge in her heart as she flattened out the piece of paper to read its inscription:

Laura,

I will be home tonight at five, at which point we need to discuss your leaving your work to come stay at home and take care of things around the house. Please be home on the time I have spoken or else we will be discussing other matters with Preacher King.

Yours.

It was hard for Laura not to crack a smile at the way he signed the note. As heartwrenching a message, his signature took her back to before they were married and he signed all his letters - not with his name or a funny anecdote, but with one small little word to prove to her that he was hers utterly. Because of his signature still finding its way onto this note, she clings to the hope that they will overcome the situation they are facing together. However... that also means she will have to tell her husband the truth.

At this exact moment of pivotal decision making, Laura is startled by a knock on the door, followed by a loving voice.

"Laura? It's Susan. I've brought Sarah with me, are you home?" Laura crossed the room to the door.

"Hello Susan, Sarah. Would you like to come in?" As the women enter into Laura's home, it is clear they notice something is off about Laura.

"Are you sure? I mean, we can come back once you've changed and fixed yourself..." Laura immediately takes her hand to her head and feels the tousled mess her hair had become. Embarrassed, she asked the woman to wait in the kitchen while she quickly through on a new outfit and wrangled her hair into a bun tucked neatly at the nape of her neck.

When she reemerged, the woman seem relieved that she has returned to her normal state.

"What brought you to my doorstep this morning? Is it labor pains? I promise it's probably just a false alarm. I've yet to be wrong about false labor."

"No, no, nothing like that. Sarah came to see me yesterday after leaving here yesterday and I wanted to come and check in to make sure that everything is alright because clearly something is going on and to be honest we are worried." Words fell from Susan's lips, quicker and more abrasive than she meant them.

"What Susan means is, are you and Ephraim okay? It just seemed so out of character for the behavior I saw yesterday..."

"We just want to know that you are okay and we want you to know that you can talk to either of us whenever you need to about anything. You have done so much for the women of this town that it seems only right that we pay it forward in their stead." Laura felt both a wave of acceptance and terror at their words of encouragement. After fifteen years of keeping her secret, could anyone forgive her? Her breaths catch in her throat as she attempts to decide whether or not she will allow them in or continue hiding her grief from more people who care about her. As she took one long inhale and exhale, she lets her gaze linger between the two women.

"What I say here does not leave here." The women sit to the front of their chairs, leaning in to see what could possibly have the strong woman they know and love so scared. "Susan, you knew me before I went away."

"We were in school together and you introduced me to my husband. I'm forever grateful you brought him into my life."

"Well, yes. But after I came back from my Rumspringa, you were the first person I went to see." Laura paused to gather thoughts. "You didn't question why I had been gone so long, you didn't tell me how much you missed me, and you didn't ask fifty questions all at once;

because the one question you did ask was enough." Susan gathered her memories in her mind to find what Laura was referring to.

"I... I asked you what happened because you looked awful. We thought that the family you had stayed with had hurt you in some way. I never really believed you when you said that they were nothing but kind to you. How could they have been when you came back looking like that?"

"What did you look like?" A perfectly innocuous question, fell on the harsh expression of Susan; letting Sarah know that it may not have been the place for that line of questioning.

"It's alright Sarah; Susan, you remember better than I do surely." Susan, annoyed at Laura's demand for her to recount a time in her life she would rather forget.

"She looked half-dead. From the bruising around her eyes, the pale white her hair had turned, the sheer loss of body weight... we were convinced you had been tortured or worse."

"In a way, I was... but not in the way you are thinking."

<u>Chapter Five</u>

Sarah and Susan stare intently at their confidant as she searches for the right way to express herself.

"Okay... so I am going to walk you through what happened to me, and I need you to just sit and listen. Please no interjections or I am not sure I will be able to make it through this." The women nod their heads in solidarity. Laura shuts her eyes and enters into her past.

*It was the third month I was in New York City. The family I was staying with took me to Times Square, this big plaza full of tourists and so many different kinds of people. It was beautiful. We went and saw a Broadway show and on our way home, I began to feel a bit off. I had been getting tired a lot recently and the pain in my stomach wasn't new either. Though I all but actually drug my heels into the ground, they took me to the hospital. After doing some tests, a tall, brooding man in a white coat came to the side of my bed. He looked stern - but that is how everyone in that world looked. I will never forget what he told me.*

*"Miss. I'm not quite sure how to tell you this, but you have end stage ovarian cancer." Though I didn't know what his words meant, I knew that it was something incredibly serious.*

*"Basically, the cancerous cells have formed cysts on your ovaries causing you the abdominal pain and the feeling of exhaustion from your body trying to fight the diseased cells. It is rare for someone of your age to have this aggressive of a strain unless you were predisposed to this condition genetically. Now, this is going to sound indelicate, however, did either your mother or grandmother have any issues like this?"*

"Did they?"

"Sarah! What did she say about interruptions?" Laura let out a wry laugh as they squabbled. When they looked up at her, Susan gestured for her to continue.

*"My mother died when I was born, and I never met my grandmother." The doctor proceeded to look at my chart, wringing his head.*

*"We need to get you booked into an ER immediately to do an emergency hysterectomy. You won't live more than six months without the operation."*

*"Don't worry Laura, we are taking care of everything. We will take care of any expense to make sure you can go back home healthier than you left."*

*"Wait... wait... what is a hysterectomy?"*

*"Well... again, I am sorry about how this sounds, but we need to go in and remove your ovarian tract because - if you want to look at your scans - there is no hope for saving them and the cancer is already beginning to spread. Unfortunately, as this procedure is highly invasive, you will have to undergo serious treatment and the recovery period could be anywhere from six months to two years." Laura's heart fell to her feet. She couldn't believe what she was being told.*

*"Okay. Well what are the long term effects of this procedure? Like, if I get it I can live a normal, healthy life?"*

*"Completely. The only thing that will be adversely affected will be that you will not be able to conceive naturally."*

"Wait a minute... you - you can't have children?" Susan's frame has shifted from the front of her chair to the back; as if all the wind had been knocked out of her.

"I fought getting the procedure... but I wasn't getting any better. And the thought of my father being here all alone, I knew I had to get better to come home to him."

"Oh my word."

"The procedure took a lot out of me, and I had to be put into this coma thing so that my body could begin to heal itself. I woke up almost eight months later; healed, but heartbroken."

"Why have you kept this from everyone? I mean, you almost died... Wait," Sarah's brain catches up with her words, "does Ephraim know?"

"No... but I feel I am going to have to tell him soon. He wants me to quit being a midwife."

"What! NO! I need you and Sarah is going to need you as her pregnancy progresses. You are the best midwife in the whole county."

"Susan, did you ever wonder why I wanted to be a midwife?"

"I just assumed that people in your family had or you just liked helping people."

"Though I do enjoy helping people on one of the most pivotal and important moments in their lives, there is a far more selfish reason I work so hard and so long with all of you. It's because when I help women deliver their babies, I am able to - just for a split second - experience the same euphoria they do and I feel less broken."

"But you aren't broken, Laura..." Sarah reaches out a hand to comfort her friend but Laura bats it away as her hot, angry tears boil over onto her cheeks.

"How would you know? Both of you have children growing in your stomachs and- and I can't have children."

"The Lord must've had a larger plan for this. I mean, you may not be able to have children, but ask any woman you have helped and they will tell you that if you hadn't been there they wouldn't be sure that they would have been able to make it through in one piece." Sarah and Susan began to cry with Laura.

"I-I just don't know how I am going to be able to tell Ephraim. I know I have to, that has become clear."

"How do you think he will react?" Susan inquires as she places her hands on Laura's.

"Why don't you turn around and ask him yourself?"

<u>Chapter Six</u>

Ephraim's gruff voice catches in his throat. Laura's eyes go wide, unable to look behind her to where his voice came from. Sarah and Susan look up to meet Ephraim's gaze, before they look back down at the terrified Laura.

"We are going to leave you two to talk." Susan stands up and grabs Sarah's wrist to guide her to the door. Sarah stalls for a second to hug Laura and only released as she whispered in her ear,

"Take a deep breath and just tell him. It will be okay." Sarah smiles as she is drug away by Susan, leaving Ephraim slouched against the door frame as Laura shrunk back into her seat. Nothing was said and no one moved for what felt like eons. Finally, because otherwise she felt she was going to go mad, Laura raised her tear stained face to ask,

"How much did you hear?"

"Every word."

"I thought you weren't going to be back until tonight."

"I... I left... well now I can't remember what I left, are we really not going to address what I just heard?"

"Look, we were fine before when you didn't know and we can be fine again. Just pretend you don't know anything and then I can go back to compartmentalizing the guilt I feel and you can go back to being angry with me or whatever you want. Just please... please pretend this didn't happen this way."

"Would you ever have told me if I didn't find out this way?" The silence between them was deafening as Laura decides that she can no longer go on lying.

"No. I wasn't. After this long, too much time had passed. And after your behavior shift a few years ago I couldn't risk you using this knowledge about me as ammunition against me to nullify our union. Because for whatever reason you are mad at me, there has not been on second, one moment since we met that I have not been completely and wholeheartedly in love with you."

"I am such a fool." Laura's sobs catch in her throat as she feels her husband approach her back and squat down in front of her to meet her gaze. "All this time I thought you were working as a midwife because you didn't want your own kids, while the whole time you have been keeping this secret from me because you were scared I would leave you? How poor a husband am I that I led you to believe that you couldn't rely on me absolutely in every aspect of your life?" Laura broke down into heart wrenching, gut punching sobs as she throws her arms around her husband. His hands pushing her closer to him, holding her tighter than he ever had before.

"I - I just couldn't live with the thought of you hating me for deceiving you for all of these years. It wasn't that I didn't want to stay home and be a housewife, it was that I couldn't stay home and be a housewife because I lack the ability to do the one thing housewives are supposed to give their husbands: children..." Laura stopped a moment to breathe, "I... I can't give you children."

"Why didn't you just talk to me about this?"

"Because I am ashamed. If not only for the fact that I accepted outside medical care, I became ashamed of my secret and it felt as if too much time had passed and I had missed my opportunity." Ephraim pulls back for a moment, taking his hand and wiping away her tears.

"I never want to hear you tell me that you are ashamed of yourself ever again. If anyone should be ashamed it is me. I didn't trust in your love for me and I didn't discuss my issues with our circumstances openly with you. I went and stewed behind your back only causing more anxiety for you and breaking our relationship even further."

"But my lies are what started it all. I am so sorry Ephraim, can you ever forgive me?"

"Laura, you are the woman I love, have always loved, and will always love. As angry and bitter as I had become, this was the last possible thing I could have conjured up to have been the reason for your neglectance to want to stay in the home."

"I love you too." Laura's sheepish confession caused Ephraim to cradle her chin in his hands, trying to find his eyes in hers. When she did finally meet his gaze, she saw something so wonderful, she thought she would never stop crying: Ephraim was smiling.

<u>Epilogue</u>

It would take much time and counseling from the elders of the community, but soon after all was revealed, Laura and Ephraim were on the path to rebuild their life together. As strong as their relationship had been, without their revelations, Laura had been sure that they would have never lasted. It has been three years since Laura was able to tell her husband the truth; and in those three years, Laura and Ephraim's relationship became strong. To show his solidarity with her work, he built her an addition on their house. In which she counseled and provided assistance to young - and oftentimes frightened - mothers-to-be; she also used the space to teach other women the skills she had acquired so she could give him the gift he wanted: more time together.

Relationships have their ebbs and flows, but trust is the stone that can either break the walls or build the castle. After their trust in eachother had been utterly destroyed by misunderstanding, it took a long time to build each other back up; and they may never finish rebuilding... But by growing together, they found that they could do anything, just so long as they had the Lord in their hearts and each other in their eyes. For God gives us nothing that we can't handle, and if it becomes too hard, He gives us each other to find solace in.

# AMISH HARVEST

## ASHLEY WOODEN

Chapter 1

Troubled Times

Jacob sat on a wooden table chair looking into the flames of the fireplace that prevented the farmhouse from getting too cold. He could hear the soft voices of his three younger sisters preparing for bed coming from upstairs. They had eaten dinner and discussed their chores and activities for the next day. Abigail, the eldest after Jacob, was to clean the house followed by feeding the livestock. The younger sisters at 15 years old were twins, Eloise and Lily; they were to also help clean the house and sew their quilts for their roadside stand. When Jacob's taxidermy business stopped bringing in the extra money lacking from the farming, they decided to establish a roadside stand down the road from their Amish settlement. All three sisters quilted when they were not taking care of the farm animals or helping around their community. In fact, their quilts were the loveliest but yet, did not attract many buyers on the road. Jacob worried about how they were going to sustain themselves and the farm in the next couple of months. They could always eat their chicken's eggs or drink milk from their cows and goats but without being able to buy feed for their animals they would starve. Jacob was feeling incompetent about struggling to provide for his family. His father was always able to provide for his wife and four children with no problems. In the middle of a thought, Abigail walked back into the kitchen ready to clean up the remnants of dinner.

"You're a bit quiet, brother," Abigail said to him as she made her way to the sink, "is everything alright?"

"Just worrying about the usual, you know?" Jacob replied with a sigh.

"God will provide, Jacob. You know that. We must have faith," Abigail encouraged him.

"Yes, I know but what am I doing wrong? With me as the man of the house, my sisters should not have to worry about finances. Father would be so disappointed in me."

"Jacob Fisher, don't you dare say such a thing. Both mother and father would be proud of you. I'm sure they are grateful for your taking on all the responsibilities after their passing. You are being much too hard on yourself. Our farm will see better days, you will see."

"I admire you for your optimism, sister."

"It is not optimism, but faith, Jacob. And faith can move mountains," Abigail continue, "You should head off to bed, big brother. We have much work to do in the early morning."

Jacob stood up from the chair and said, "Thank you for your encouraging words, Abigail. I will not let you or Eloise or Lily down. That is a promise! Have a good night, sister." Jacob made his way up the stairs to his bedroom where he eventually dozed off while trying to come to a solution to their financial hardship.

The next morning Eloise, Lily, and Jacob set off down the road with the quilts that were ready to be sold for the day. Eloise and Lily could have gone to the stand alone or with Abigail but Jacob did not feel comfortable with his sisters being alone out by the road. He was concerned that they would get hit by a car or that someone would attempt to mug them. Those were chances he was not willing to take. They exited the settlement's wooden fence and walked the mile down the road carrying their quilts in boxes. Eloise and Lily spent much of their time designing their quilts and piecing them together. Any spare time they got after finishing their chores was spent on the quilts. Jacob always wished he was as creative as they; they seemed to have a more colorful view of the world. He loved that about his sisters. Once they set up the wooden stand with their prepared merchandise, they waited for their first customer of the day. Usually, on a good day, they'd sell at least 4 of the 10 quilts they had prepared. The quilts although very intricate, were not sold for much money as Jacob felt guilty of capitalizing on his younger sisters' hard work. They also could not produce more than they were already, as it was just them two, Eloise and Lily, making them with the rare help of Abigail who was mostly busy with cooking, cleaning and helping Jacob tend to the farm.

The siblings were conversing about the weather when they noticed a red car slowed down and a woman, who appeared to be in her early twenties, rolled down her window as she passed. She drove a few more feet and pulled over to the side of the road. She exited her car and walked over to view the quilts on display. The woman inspected the quilts intently without saying a word.

"May I touch one?" she asked politely.

"Yes, ma'am," Jacob replied.

"Who makes these?" the woman asked.

"We do," Eloise and Lily answered proudly.

"Wow, these are so beautiful, girls. I love the colors and they are soft to the touch. I bet these come in handy during the cold winter, huh?"

"Oh, yes," Lily said, "but they are also good for the warmer months, too. They are very lightweight."

"How much do they run for?" The woman was amazed when she heard how little they charged for the quilts.

"You're kidding me. These are much higher quality than the expensive ones I've bought at department stores. I'm impressed!"

"I'll take these three, please," she said indicating which ones she chose with her index finger. Eloise and Lily loved the sound of that and smiled at each other. They were so excited about the sale that they seemed to have forgotten about the woman standing there. Jacob grabbed their shoulders and said, "Well, sisters, your kind customer is waiting for her quilts."

"Oh, yes! Sorry, ma'am. We usually don't sell so many at a time," Eloise exclaimed, already taking care of the transaction.

"That's a shame," the woman said, "these quilts are so intricate and lovely. My mother is going to love hers. She hates the paper-thin plain sheets they give her at the nursing home."

"A nursing home?" Lily asked. Jacob looked at her wide-eyed hoping the woman would not be offended by Lily's innocent curiosity.

"Yes, you know where they take care of elderly or ill people," the woman replied.

"Huh," Lily replied, "we don't have any of those at our community. Why don't you just take care of her yourself?"

"Lily!" Jacob exclaimed.

The woman held up her hands and waved shaking her head, "No, no don't worry," she said to Jacob, "that's a valid question." The woman went on to explain about how her mother had recently taken a fall off the front porch and broken her hip. She was in the process of finding a caregiver to look after her mother while she worked.

"Sorry about your mother," Jacob said to the woman.

"Thank you," the woman replied.

"What is your job?" Eloise asked.

"Girls, what is with all of the questions. I'm sure the lady has somewhere to be right now. I'm so sorry," he apologized to the woman who laughed.

"It's okay. I have some time to kill before visiting hours at the nursing home. I'm Annie, by the way. What are your names?"

"I am Jacob and these are my two teenage sisters, Eloise and Lily," Jacob answered.

"Nice to meet you, Jacob, Eloise and Lily. To answer your question, I'm a tax accountant."

"Oh? You must be very business-oriented," Jacob said.

"I sure am," Annie replied.

"I thought you would be a model of some sort," Eloise chimed in.

"Oh, stop it," Annie chuckled. Jacob would have thought so, too. He analyzed her facial features—soft, yet bold. Her skin was fair and flawless and her brunette hair was healthy-looking as well.

"You know, you have a really pretty face," Lily said to Annie.

"You two are the cutest twins I have ever met," Annie told them chuckling.

"So, listen," Annie added, "If you ever need help with your taxes or if you have any business inquiries please call me. I'm not sure if you're allowed to but just in case." Annie took out a business card from her wallet and handed it to Jacob.

"Thank you for stopping by," Jacob told her with the girls nodding beside him in agreeance and they looked on as Annie walked back to her car. The siblings' day had been made by their encounter with Annie and her appreciation for the quilts they love to make. Jacob, however, could not stop thinking that maybe there was another reason for their encounter, after all, she was an accountant.

Chapter Two

Help Arrives

"I don't know, Jacob. I'm not sure about how I feel about an outsider coming to help us," Abigail responded to Jacob's proposition.

"We need help, Abigail. I think Annie is the answer to our problems with the farm," Jacob told her.

"What will our community say? I will not consider it, brother. I am sorry but no. Besides, how do we even know if this woman knows what she is doing? You said she was young, recently graduated and such. What if she worsens our problems?"

"We won't know until we try, Abigail. I'm sure others won't be bothered by her presence here. She will only be here to help. Just say the word and I will give her a call."

"Please, sister. Let's call Annie for help." Eloise and Lily both pleaded.

"You too?" Abigail asked.

"She's a very nice lady. You will like her, too," Lily said to Abigail.

"Are you not the one who told me to have more faith, Abigail? I have faith that God will help us through our hardships but I also believe that maybe he has sent Annie to help." Abigail could not refute that. It had been months since she saw Jacob be so hopeful about something. While her concern about the rest of the Amish community's opinion about Annie's presence there would bother her, she also did not want her brother in despair either. She looked at her brother's worried expression and could not turn down his pleading eyes.

"Okay," Abigail agreed reluctantly, "but if our farm doesn't start doing better we must not let her linger here."

"I trust this woman," Jacob said, "and I trust God, too." Later on that day, he called Annie and asked her to come by later in the day to discuss business about the farm. Annie excitedly agreed to be there for dinner. The siblings were excited at the prospect of someone coming to rescue the farm; with the exception of Abigail who was still hesitant to accept help outside of their settlement. There were so many improvements to be made but Annie gave off a sense of confidence with her profession that the Fisher's just had to give her a chance.

When the dinner hour came by and there was no sign of Annie, the sisters were convinced that she was a no-show.

"This is why we shouldn't try outsiders," Abigail said.

"She should have just said she didn't want to help," Eloise chimed in disappointedly.

"Sisters, I don't truly believe that kind Annie would leave us hanging out to dry like this. I'm going to go out and look for her. Maybe she is having car troubles or she's lost," Jacob said as he grabbed a jacket from their coat hanger to go out in the night. Abigail tried to convince him that he was not going to find Annie out there but Jacob would hear nothing of it. Jacob walked over to their horse who was grazing next to the farmhouse and mounted it. He went towards the entrance of the settlement and saw what looked like headlights. Annie was standing by her car with some men from the settlement blocking her entrance.

"Hey!" Jacob yelled, "is something the matter?" He asked as he got closer. The three men blocking Annie from entering were of the older and more respectable men of the settlement.

"This strange woman is trying to trespass into our property," one of the men said.

"Oh, no. She's no stranger. She is an accountant who offered to help our farm," Jacob explained.

"You went outside for help? What about our accountant who is part of our community?" The old man asked.

"I apologize, gentlemen. I mean no disrespect; I only mean to seek for a way in which I can properly sustain my family and our farm. As you know, I have already gone to our accountant for help but have not had any success," Jacob replied.

"So you mean to say that our members are incompetent?"

"Not at all, sir. I simply wanted the opinion of someone who had experience in the outside business world. I do not mean to offend anybody."

"Very well," the older man said, "she may enter. But the car stays out of our fields."

As the men made their way back to their buggy, Jacob said, "I'm so sorry Annie. I did not know they would react that way. Our settlement is very strict on our interactions with the world outside of our settlement. They do not want our people to be influenced by outsiders. My apologies."

"No worries. I respect everyone's views and practices—no need to apologize," Annie told him although, she was not happy with the way the older men had treated her; as if she was a person who meant to do harm. She decided to not express her feelings on the incident, however, because she did not want to disrespect Jacob or his sisters in doing so.

Annie had to park her car outside, by the side of the road. Jacob offered to let her sit on the horse since it was a half-mile walk back to the farmhouse but she was not an experienced rider so they went back by foot, instead. On their way back, Jacob told her about his sister being a bit reluctant to accept help from a stranger. Annie took no offense to it as she understood that they rarely had any contact with outsiders and after her encounter earlier, she was sure that it was looked down upon by the rest of the community as well.

"Don't worry though, Annie. I assure you, we are peaceful people. You will not be attacked or anything of the sort," Jacob reassured her.

"Okay, I trust you," Annie smiled. Jacob had never seen such a white, radiant smile before. Annie's smile lit up her entire face. It was a sight he very much enjoyed.

When they arrived at the farmhouse, the sisters were waiting on the porch.

"Hello, Annie!" Eloise and Lily called out.

"Hi, girls," Annie replied walking up the steps.

"You must be Abigail," Annie said holding out her hand for a shake. Abigail hesitated for a moment but eventually shook Annie's hand.

"Yes, hello. We are glad you were able to make it," Abigail told her.

"Were you lost?" Lily asked. Jacob went on to tell them about Annie's encounter with the older men by the entrance.

"Sorry about that," Abigail said, "why don't we get straight to business?" Abigail was glad that someone was willing to help her brother but did not wish Annie to stay longer for fear of people treating them differently.

The Fisher siblings and Annie all sat down at the table and talked while Abigail served dinner. Eloise and Lily told Annie about their farm animals and told her funny stories. Jacob enjoyed seeing his sisters conversing with Annie so well. One would not even think that the twins were Amish from looking at how comfortably they interacted with a person who was not Amish like themselves. Annie had never eaten Amish dishes so she was excited. In the middle of dinner, there was a small moment of quietness because everybody was enjoying Abigail's cooking so much. Once they were all finished and the sisters had cleared the table, Annie took out her portfolio and began to take notes. Jacob told her about the sales from their farming, the money they made from his taxidermy and the girls' quilts, and many other things to give her a clear understanding of their financial situation. Annie ran some numbers and wrote down notes on her pages. She was focused and worked quickly. After about an hour of exchanging information, Annie said she had a plan. She went ahead and laid out a budget plan for them. They were to spend just enough money on the care of their livestock but in order to save a little bit more money, they were to stop buying fabric for the quilts and materials for Jacob's taxidermy.

"No quilting? Must we really stop?" Eloise whined.

"If you want to save a little bit of money, then yes. But hopefully, if we can start getting your farm to a point where you are no longer losing money, you can start quilting again. It's only for a short while, I promise. We are going to turn this farm around!"

"Can we save enough money to acquire more livestock and grow our farming business?"

"Yes, definitely," Annie replied, "but maybe not for the moment. What we can also do is expand the products you offer. For example, instead of selling milk, butter, and eggs; you can also grow a garden and sell your produce."

"A garden? That's a fantastic idea. We can grow flowers, too! We can sell them at our stand along with our quilts," Lily said excitedly.

"I like that idea, too," Annie said.

They spent hours talking about what steps they were going to take to get their farming business to a sustainable level. The more the siblings spoke with Annie, the more they liked her—even Abigail. Jacob admired how knowledgeable she was about business at her young age. She displayed not an ounce of intimidation. Annie also took a liking to the Fisher sibling as they were a very tight-knit group. They had a bond with each other that she never had the chance to form as she was an only child.

Chapter Three

Growth and Goodbyes

Over the next few months, the Fisher farm improved drastically. Annie was able to negotiate for two more cows, which allowed them to collect more milk which also meant more butter. They started using the extra milk to make cream as well. It took a lot of work and many hours of labor but the farm was finally attracting other members to buy from them. Abigail had the idea of also planting herbs for medicine or cooking. Soon, their farm became the primary place for the settlement's grocery needs. The siblings had so much to be grateful for towards Anne. It had been years since the family hadn't a burden to carry upon their shoulders. While the Amish members did grow to love the new farm, they were not always very welcoming to Annie. A few times, the older women of the settlement attempted to shame her during her visits for being unmarried or for saying that her wardrobe was not modest enough to be around their community. Annie did not let it bother her, however. She did not even think that the women were rude for saying things like that, after all, they were from completely different worlds and led different lifestyles. She understood that they were just not used to outside culture.

Jacob and Annie had been spending an extensive amount of time together during those months as well. It never really dawned on either of them that Annie's help had been accomplished and that her job there was done. By the time that the farm was successfully bringing in money, they had begun to spend more time doing things besides work. The twins had begun to teach her about quilting, Abigail had taught her how to tend to the livestock and comically, Jacob had taught her how to play the game of horseshoes. One evening as they were playing out in the field, Annie tripped into a pothole and let out a yell.

Jacob broke into a run and bent down beside her. "Are you okay?" he asked.

"I think so. I believe I've twisted my ankle," she lamented.

"Can you walk on it?" Jacob asked. Annie tried to stand but her ankle was unable to support her weight and she began to fall again before Jacob grabbed her by the waist. In all of the months they had worked together, not once had they ever touched—not even for a handshake. The feeling made them pause for a minute, processing what had happened. It felt so foreign to the two of them; especially to Jacob who had never touched a person of the opposite sex before. Although, something made him glad that Annie was the first woman he'd touched, even in this innocent scenario. Through Annie, his sisters had gained a newfound confidence and had learned many things they would not have learned in the settlement. After all, the school system only allows for the children to attend school for up to the eighth grade. For that, Jacob really appreciated her.

"I think I'll have to carry you back to the farmhouse. Is that alright with you?"

"Yes, thank you." On their way to the farmhouse, many of the Amish members stared them down with reactions varying from utter shock and horror to anger and disgust. When they arrived at the house, Jacob set her down on the porch. Soon, the same older man who tried to impede Annie from entering the settlement months ago walked up to the Fisher's porch. The two other men were also alongside him.

"Jacob Fisher, are you courting this outsider?"

"No, sir. Not at all."

"What is the meaning of this? Why are you touching this woman in this manner?"

"This manner? Our friend Annie was hurt out in the field and is unable to walk. I was simply trying to bring her to safety."

"You should have asked one of our women to carry her or your sisters. This is unacceptable. This woman has overextended her stay. She must leave at once. We do not want her influencing our people any longer."

"How can you be so harsh? She saved our farm and by doing so has also helped our community develop new resources for food."

"Jacob, it's okay. I will go inside to get my things and be on my way," Annie said to Jacob. She turned to the elder man and said, "I apologize if my presence has made you uncomfortable in your own home. I promise you to stay away from now on." Annie then limped into the house to gather her belongings and say goodbye to the Fisher sisters.

"Annie, I'm so sorry," Jacob called behind her as he walked through the front door.

"No, it's okay. Really. I got too comfortable here when I shouldn't have. That was impolite of me. I should be the one who is sorry. I got you in trouble," Annie told him.

"Please, let me at least bandage up your ankle before you go. I can't let you leave injured like that," Jacob pleaded.

"Okay," Annie said with a sad smile. They settled in the bathroom where they kept their First Aid supplies in a cabinet. Annie sat on the toilet while Jacob sat across from her on the edge of the bathtub with her foot in his lap.

"It looks like you might have to go to the hospital," Jacob said, pointing to her purple and swollen ankle. Jacob bandaged up her foot slowly, taking in all the time they had left together.

"Where are your parents?" Annie asked suddenly, "I'm sorry. I've been curious about it."

"It's okay. I'll tell you for old time's sake," he chuckled. "Well, one night my parents were on the buggy on the road. A drunk truck driver hit them from behind and they died instantaneously. Ironically, the horse survived."

"I'm so sorry," Annie said, "You know, your parents would be proud of how well you've managed to take care of your sisters."

"I couldn't have done anything without your help, Annie. Thank you, forever. We will always be grateful to you for that. I'm so sorry about how the people of this community have treated you," Jacob told her. When everything was all said and done, Jacob helped her up on the horse and led her to her car which she had always parked on the side of the road. They walked in silence, not wanting to make the moment sadder. Annie had not a chance to say goodbye to the Fisher sisters as they were joining in other activities with the women. She was really sad about that. They were unable to look at each other for the length of their walk for fear of crying to each other. Jacob was feeling a mixture of emotions, he felt angry at the unfairness of Annie's treatment. He was saddened by how a nice person like herself could be banished so harshly. Once they reached the road, Jacob helped Annie into her car and she rolled down her window.

"Please say goodbye to your sisters for me," Annie told him, "Maybe once I get better I'll come by the stand to buy some quilts and flowers."

"Yes, they would love that," Jacob said, "And I would, too. Thank you—for everything."

"I wish you all the luck and prosperity for you and your sisters," Annie said sadly. She felt the warmth of her tears starting to collect in her eyes so she quickly rolled up the window and started the car. Jacob and Annie waved goodbye. As Annie drove off, she silently cried for the boy who would never be part of her world.

Chapter Four

New Beginnings

Weeks passed after Annie's departure and they had not heard from her. Abigail thought it was for the best, even though, she missed her girl talks with Annie. Eloise and Lily would look for her car on the road as they worked at the stand, but they never did see her. Jacob had become a moping man—going on horse rides all alone, refusing to eat, and even refusing to work. His sisters had noticed the changes in his mood but were too embarrassed to ask. They had all come to love Annie and truthfully, would not be surprised if their older brother had actually fallen in love with her. One night, as the Fisher's sat at the dinner table, Abigail observed her brother's face. He had atrocious dark circles and could tell he was unwell. He fiddled with his food, poking it around with his fork but not taking any bites.

"Jacob Fisher, what is the matter with you?" Abigail demanded.

"What?" Jacob said quietly as he looked up from his plate.

"You heard me. What is wrong with you? You were so happy and now look at you. You're walking around like a gray man."

"I think I may be ill," Jacob responded.

"Lovesick, you mean?" Lily asked. Jacob turned his head to look at her, kind of bothered that she had asked but his eyes couldn't lie.

"We know," Abigail revealed to him, "you're not very good at hiding that, brother."

"We miss Annie, too," Eloise said. Jacob remained quiet simply looking at his sister's' faces.

"I'm not sure about what you want to hear from me," Jacob said.

"Tell me, brother. Honestly, can you eventually get over this or is this the person you'll remain?" Abigail asked her brother seriously.

"I don't know. It's been weeks and I still look for her car on the road. I can still hear her voice when I'm out in the fields. Every time I shut my eyes to sleep, her face resurges from my memory. I thought that I was happy because our farm was doing so well and I am glad for that. But, when she left I realized that I was only happy because she was here. She was always so open, so free-spirited. It was so foreign to us. I thought maybe I was just infatuated."

"What are you going to do about it, then?" Abigail asked him.

"I can do nothing else but live with it. There is no way we could ever be together. An Amish lifestyle would not suit her," Jacob lamented. Abigail was heartbroken to see her brother that way, as well as Eloise and Lily. It had been a very long time since they had seen Jacob so deflated. Even during the months that their farm had been doing bad, he was still energetic. The most vivacious they'd ever seen Jacob was when Annie was helping them daily. They were baffled with how they could have possibly missed it.

"Brother, I have to ask you something. Please, remain level-headed and I do apologize if my question seems ridiculous or even disrespectful. Would we be suited to live on the outside? Where she is?" Abigail asked cautiously. Eloise and Lily exchanged glances with a glimmer of curiosity and excitement in their eyes.

"What do you mean to tell me, Abigail?"

"Please don't be upset by my reply. What I mean is what if we renounce the Amish lifestyle and try to make it outside of here?"

"Do you mean that?" Jacob asked.

"I do. Knowing mother and father, I know they would want you to live your life with the person you loved the most—just like they did with each other. You have done enough for our family and our farm. You should be with who makes you happy whether it's out there or in this settlement. Just be happy."

"Would we be able to go to a regular school?" Eloise asked with excitement.

"Oh, please do let us," Lily cried. A smile from Jacob's lips appeared after weeks of it being absent.

"Would you be willing? How can you leave behind our life like that? Not that I have any objection," Jacob asked.

"Annie is a wonderful person. I oftentimes found myself fantasizing about what life would be like if I had her daily life. I, truthfully, would like to give jeans a try." The siblings broke out into wild laughter from Abigail's confession.

"Actually, so do we," Eloise confessed and Lily nodded.

"Is this what we truly want?" He asked his sisters. The three girls nodded their heads.

Jacob laughed from the relief and the hope his sisters had given him. They all joined in a group hug and began to discuss their game plan.

Weeks after the Fisher's life-changing decision, Annie still had yet to contact them. She sat in her office at work when her phone rang. It was her receptionist letting her know she had a few visitors. Annie told her to lead them to her office. The receptionist cracked the door open to let the visitors in. To Annie's surprise, it was Jacob and his sisters. Annie sat there stunned from their unexpected visit.

"Oh my gosh, hi," she finally cried, "what are you guys doing here?" She stood up from her desk and walked over to hug each of the siblings but before she could hug any of them, Jacob got in her way and planted a kiss on her lips. Annie wrapped her arms around Jacob and hugged him. After some moments, the girls all started ooh-ing in a juvenile manner. As they pulled apart from each other, Jacob held up a bouquet of their newly bloomed white roses.

"I picked these out for you, from our garden," he said. Annie just stood there without saying a word. For a minute, Jacob was afraid that he had made a mistake in kissing her. He was so glad to see her that he forgot to ask. He was feeling beyond nervous at that moment.

"Oh, I'm so sorry, Annie. I shouldn't have done that. I didn't mean to disrespect you," Jacob apologized.

Annie shook her head, "No, Jacob, that was great. Truly, super appreciated. I don't understand what is going on. Why are you here?"

"We left the Amish settlement," Eloise said.

"Like, to visit?" Annie said.

"No, silly," Lily told her, "We live out here now."

"Is this true, Jacob?" Annie asked in disbelief. Jacob nodded his head. The siblings went ahead and explained all of the events that took place in the weeks prior to their visit. They told her all about how they had saved enough money to survive outside of the settlement since the farm had done so exceptionally well thanks to her help. They also revealed to her that they had left another family in charge of their Amish farm while they found someone who was willing to buy it. The twins were excited about enrolling in high school soon and asked Annie if she was willing to help them go clothes and school supply shopping. The Fisher family was very excited about the beginning of their new life.

The people of the settlement did not agree with them leaving their home for the sake of an outsider but there was no changing the Fisher's minds, especially Jacob. The Amish lifestyle, while simple and humble, was not what they wished to live for the rest of their lives. There was nothing wrong with being of the Amish world, but Annie had shown them just a fraction of the beautiful world she was a part of and they wanted to be there with her, too.

"Why would you guys do that?" Annie asked.

"Because we like you," Eloise said.

"And because our brother loves you," Abigail said. Annie looked over at Jacob who was now quiet. Annie wanted to hear it from him.

"This is true," Jacob confessed, "At first, I had no idea what these feelings were. I thought what I felt was immense gratitude for all you have done for us. After you were told to never step foot in the settlement, I realized that in the process of bringing the farm back to life I had fallen in love with you. I am in love with you, Annie."

By that point, all the girls in the room were crying, including Annie who had believed their connection to be impossible. Clearly, it was not.

"I was so afraid of telling you how I felt because it was pointless," Annie said, "They had issues with you bringing in a non-Amish person for business purposes; I can't imagine their reaction to you being involved romantically with one. I didn't want to bring you problems. I would have never thought that you would ever leave just to be here, with me."

"What is meant to be, will always find a way," Abigail said. Jacob knew that his parents would be happy with their decision and he was proud of their courage and bravery to set upon this journey.

The following months consisted of many trips of discovery and exploration of the world outside Amish walls. With the money they earned from the sale of their previous farm, they were eventually able to buy a new plot of farmland since all of them, including Annie, missed farming. Annie even showed Abigail and the twins the power of the internet and helped them start their online shop for customized quilts. It was still a life-altering change that they set upon and times were not always easy, neither were adjustments. But, just like back at the farm, Annie always found a way to comfort them and brought them peace no matter the challenge. There was also the fact that Jacob and Annie were madly in love, and that always gave them the courage to face everything with bravery and positivity.

"Do you ever regret leaving the settlement?" Annie asked Jacob one night while they cuddled on her living room couch.

"Not at all. I love being with you and my sisters do, too. Although, it is a bit more complicated out here; I try not to worry so much even though we get scared. There are many things we are not used to but you're a good example of how to keep it together when things around you get crazy. You're good at that, you know?"

"Well, I'm glad I was able to make such an impact in your guy's' life. I'm also glad I didn't lose you," Annie replied as she rested her head on his shoulder.

"Never," Jacob replied, kissing the top of her head. Just like that, the pain from the time they were apart was forgotten and became a thing of the past.

# LONE MOON RANCH



## PART ONE

She felt a mix of relief and despair as she watched the Boston skyline fade away. She felt a mix of relief and despair. She knew she would never come back to her beloved hometown. There was nothing left for her there. In fact, all she had left fit into a small carry-on bag. Her life had shattered, and most of the pieces had blown away in the wind.

She grabbed her phone and read Colt's email again.

*I am a simple man. I own the Lone Moon Ranch in Helena, Montana. I've lived here all my life. I am 26 now. I am looking for a wife, someone who can take over the household duties; cooking, cleaning and such. Also, to assist with various chores around the ranch. I need someone who is not deterred by early mornings and not afraid of hard work. In return, I will make sure you are well-taken care of. I am seeking a partner, not a companion. Please contact me if you have questions.*

He didn't include a photo and she never asked for one. It didn't matter what he looked like. She appreciated the fact that he sounded very businesslike in his email. That's what this was – a business deal. She had placed an ad on a mail order bride site - not for love, but for security. Colt fit the bill. He needed a wife and she needed an escape. Of course, he had no clue what she was escaping from. She hadn't been completely honest with him about her past.

She tossed her phone back into her purse. She rubbed her thumb against her ring finger as she laid back against her seat and closed her eyes. She didn't want to think about Nick. But he was always there, lurking just below the surface. She could picture his dark eyes and dangerous smile. When they met, he made her feel alive and invincible. Loving Nick was like grabbing hold of a lightning bolt. He had lit her up and then burned her to ashes.

They got married a month after their first date. Nick was wild and impulsive that way, and she couldn't deny him anything. But Nick was also a drunk and a gambler. He got so wasted on their wedding night that he passed out in the hotel lobby. Three months in, he had blown through all her savings. He became violent and erratic when the money ran out. He isolated her from her family and her friends so she had no one to help her. And she couldn't leave him. They were each other's obsession even though he scared her. But then one night he crashed into another car and almost killed the driver. She could picture his face the day of sentencing. Six years. And the way he looked at her the last time she went to visit him, to tell him she had filed for divorce. She lied to him and told him it was all his fault. But she couldn't lie to herself. She knew she was just as much to blame. Maybe he struck the match but they had both danced within the flames.

Their 2-year marriage had stripped her of everything. She lost her condo, her car, and even her job. Her parents had both passed way, and both her brother and sister had given up on her. She needed to start over. And there were worst ways to do that than a beautiful ranch in Montana. So, she bought a plane ticket and a new dress using the only credit card she had left and swore to do her very best to not look back.

****

Colt Malone stood inside Helena Regional Airport. He jiggled his truck keys impatiently against his thigh. Joelle's flight had been delayed. And while he was many things, patient was not one of them. It was a trait that had never come easily to him. Mainly because he rarely liked to be idle.

Nearly every woman that walked past him, smiled. Women had always noticed him. But it had been a long time since one had shared his life or his bed. Not since Ashlyn. They had grown up together. He chased her from the moment he was big enough to run. He couldn't recall a moment of his life that he didn't love her. She had been his best friend and then his lover. But Ashlyn wanted to chase something of her own. Her dreams had taken her far from Montana and far from him. She was in California now. He used to think they'd get married and build a life together. He used to think love matter more than anything. Now he knew better. Love broke you in ways that would never heal. And he didn't intend to ever give someone that kind of power over him again.

He made the ranch his whole life. His father had died three years prior, and he had no other family. When his father died, the ranch and all the responsibility of it became his. It was a huge undertaking. The ranch was financially in bad shape. It was burden his father had never shared with him, but something he inherited just the same.

Things still weren't great. He worked from sun up to sun down, but the ranch was still in jeopardy. He had to lay off most of the staff. He had taken out new loans to pay off old ones. But the ranch was still in debt. He knew he didn't have time to be angry but he was. He was angry that his father hadn't been a better businessman. He was angry at his mother for leaving when he was young. He was angry at the hand life and love had dealt him.

He couldn't say what came over him the night he went online and found the mail order bride website. He guessed it was his loneliness. He wanted to come home to a hot meal and a warm body. He didn't want someone to fall in love with but he did want a partner. Someone to share his burdens and his life. Joelle's ad had stood out to him. She was beautiful but haunted. Long, dark hair and big expressive eyes. She looked like a painting from another time and place. She seemed like a woman that could possess a man and make him beg at her feet, and yet gave him the sense that she didn't want to possess anyone. What she wanted was security. A place in the world that belonged to her. He could give her that, even if he could never give her his heart.

The gate opened, and a rush of people came toward him. Cole scanned the crowd looking for her. He had looked at her picture a dozen times. He had stared into her hazel eyes and memorized the color of her lips and the curve of her neck. His finger had traced each wave of her long, raven hair. But that picture had in no way prepared him for the real-life version.

He called her name and she walked toward him, her cheeks flush and her hair slightly tangled. She was smiling, but it didn't quite reach her eyes.

"Colt?"

"Hello," he said. His voice came out slightly gruff.

"Hi." She hesitated for a moment, but then sat down her bag and leaned into him.

He didn't think, he just put his arms around her and closed his eyes. He felt his whole body respond to hers, full and warm against him. She smelled of a lavender and citrus. And when she pulled back to look up at him, he felt breathless for the first time in a long time. Yep, she could awaken a hunger in a man and he was in no way immune; and it was a hunger he had almost forgotten was there. His pulse quickened, and this animal desire to ravage her was stirring inside. He swallowed, and took a long, shaky breath.

"I'm glad I'm here," she said softly.

"So am I."

They stood for a moment, still half in each other's arm. He took another breath and steadied himself.

"We should get going Do you have more bags?" he asked.

She smiled again in a sad sort of way. He saw something in her eyes for the briefest of moments, but then it was gone.

"This is all I have." She gestured toward the bag at her feet. "I meant it when I said I was looking forward to a fresh start."

He picked up the bag for her. "My trucks just outside then," he said. "We have an appointment at the courthouse in less than an hour."

She nodded. They had done the paperwork online, and obtain their marriage license. He had told her he didn't see any reason to put things off, and so he made an appointment at the courthouse for them to be married that afternoon. She didn't seem to want to wait either.

They exited the airport and Joelle's breath hitched as she took in the landscape. The blue sky was cloudless and seemed to have no end. The land before them was flat and rugged until your eyes found the mountains jutting into the heavens.

"It's so beautiful," she said softly.

"It is," he agreed. He had never strayed far from home. The soul of him came from the land and those mountains.

They reached his pickup truck, and he tossed her bag into the bed of it. The truck was painted a fire engine red and it was well loved and taken care of.

"After you." He opened the passenger side door, and then without thinking he reached down and touched her cheek. This made her lips part slightly.

An invitation?

Her lips were as red as his truck and he couldn't seem to look away. Slowly he bent down, letting his own lips graze her's. His hands fell to her waist, and he pulled her body to his. He kissed her, tasting the sweetness of her. She didn't respond to him at first. But he felt the exact moment when she let go. She molded herself to him, and her body hummed. She made a sexy, breathy sound and it about did him in. Somehow he knew she had the same kind of demons that he did. She buried things too. Maybe like him, she still held out hope that one day she'd find redemption.

She pulled away first. She stared at him, her breath ragged.

"Colt, I didn't come here to fall for you."

Trying to regain his composure he said, "I didn't bring you here to fall in love."

"Before we do this, I need you to promise me again. Love is not part of the agreement."

"I do. And I'll keep my promise." He nodded toward the open truck door and ran his fingers through his hair. She was holding his gaze, searching.

"So will I," she said and got up into the truck. They were on the road a moment later, heading for the courthouse on the other side of town.

***

Joelle tried to stop her hands from shaking. She and Colt had arrived at the courthouse, and she could hear the Judge and Colt talking. But all she could think of was that moment she spotted him in the airport. He had on a pair of Wrangler's that fit him well and a button-down shirt. Cowboy boots of course and she had spotted a matching cowboy hat in the truck. He was also sporting a five o'clock shadow even though it was only noon. He wore it well. Too well. He was quite possibly the most handsome man she had even laid eyes on. His auburn hair that curled at the ends and those smoky eyes rimmed with lashes that went on for days. And when he kissed her...

"We're ready." Colt touched her arm lightly. The Judge was just beside him.

"But are you ready my dear?" he asked. He had a soft voice and a kindly face.

"I do – I mean I am," she stammered. They both smiled at her and she laughed nervously. Colt had her undone and that was not part of the plan.

The simple ceremony took less than ten minutes. When it concluded, Colt leaned in and kissed her again. This kiss was softer and sweeter. It held a promise instead of passion. It told her he would be there and he would take care of her.

"Let's go home," he said.

It was a good twenty minutes before they reached the ranch. Colt turned down a rocky drive. Lone Moon Ranch sat a mile off the main road with rolling hills on either side. The main house was average in size, painted red with a white a trim. A barn sat directly to the left of the house, and acres of pasture and field to the right. She breathed in the smell of cut grass and watched as hundreds of dandelions danced in the late afternoon breeze. She spotted several cows in the pasture, and could make out the sound of horses nearby.

He put the car in park right in front of the house. He got out and came around to open the door for her. They stood in the driveway for a long time in silence. He was letting her take everything in. She had never seen so much land and beauty in all her life. She felt like she had been dropped in the middle of nowhere, and the middle of nowhere looked a lot like paradise.

"Hello!" A middle-aged woman came down the front porch steps. She was drying her hands on the apron she wore. Her graying hair was pulled back into a tight bun, and she had a big smile on her face. She came toward Joelle, and pulled her into a tight hug.

"My goodness, you are gorgeous." She pulled back, holding Joelle at arm's length. Then she leaned in and hugged her again. "We are so happy to have you. And congratulations to you both!" She turned to him then, and he bent so she could kiss his cheek. She looked at him with such affection that it made Joelle smile.

"This is Minnie," Colt said. "Minnie, this is Joelle."

"You can call me Jo."

Minnie turned back and hugged her again.

"Minnie is a dear friend," he explained. "She comes by once or twice a week to help tidy up or cook one of her delicious meals. I don't deserve her at all, but I honestly don't know what I would do without her."

"Oh shush." She slapped him playfully on the arm. "I love you like my own son. And how I wish I could do more for you, love." Her eyes got misty. "But here you are now." She turned back to Joelle. "I am just so happy that Colt has found someone to love again."

Colt cleared his throat uncomfortably and she got the impression that Minnie had no idea how they had met. And maybe she would be a bit taken aback if she knew he had basically gone online and ordered up a bride.

"Well, I am happy to be here. So happy," Joelle said. "Colt has just stolen my heart and I don't ever want it back."

Minnie clapped her hands in delight, smiling brightly at them. He was giving her a look, and she gave him a sideways smile.

"Well, come on in. You must be tired and famished. I have dinner all ready." She directed them inside, like a shepherd herding her flock.

Once inside the house, she took a moment to look around her new home. All the rooms were big and open, with high ceilings and lots of windows. The living room was to her left, and a large stone fireplace stood against the back wall. He didn't have a whole lot of furniture, a leather couch, and two big chairs.

She made her way to the kitchen, which was also airy and full of lots of natural light. A large island sat in the center and a small breakfast nook in the corner. The dining room sat off to the right, and both rooms blended well together.

"There's a roast warming in the oven. And biscuits on the table," Minnie said. "You've outdone yourself again," he told her.

"Oh, don't fuss on me. You sit down and enjoy your dinner. I'll be around tomorrow, Jo, to help you settle in."

"Thank you – so much," she said.

Minnie smiled and touched her cheek. "You're going to be very happy here," she promised and then she was gone.

He glanced toward the dining room table. "Shall we?" he asked.

She nodded, her stomach rumbling at the thought. She hadn't eaten breakfast or lunch that day. In fact, she hadn't eaten much at all lately. Certainly, nothing that resembled a home cooked meal.

They ate in silence for several minutes. She savored the biscuits dipped in honey. She glanced up at him, the late afternoon sun poured in through a window, and she could see the flecks of red in his hair.

"I'm sorry you didn't have any family or friends here today," he said.

"I don't have a family. None that speak to me anyway. And no real friends either," she told him. "It's just me."

"Why doesn't your family speak to you?" he asked.

She looked up, meeting his gaze. "My parents died last year. It was a car accident. That sent my spiraling a bit. I didn't always make the best decisions. My brother and sister are both older than me. I guess they handle things better than I do. She has two kids and he owns his own business. I'm the black sheep and they finally threw in the towel."

"Doesn't seem fair," he said. "You're family. They shouldn't just turn their backs on you."

"I don't blame them," she replied honestly. "I hurt them a lot. They felt like they needed to protect themselves."

He sat back in his chair, holding her gaze across the table. "Is that why you left? Why you married me?"

"I don't have anything, Colt. I'm embarrassed to say that, but it's the truth. But now I'm your wife. And here we are together, and I want this to work. I want this ranch to be as much mine as it is yours. I want us to take care of it together."

"And you mean that?"

"I do."

"You know, it's just me, too. Sure – I have friends. Wonderful friends. But no family. This ranch is all I have, and I work every day to hold on to it for me... For us." He paused still watching her. "And I'm sorry about your parents. I never knew my mother, but my daddy passed away three years ago. So, I mean it – I am sorry."

"It's been over a year. You would think it would hurt a little less by now."

"It won't ever hurt any less. You just learn to live with it."

They took their time finishing dinner. She liked talking to him and he seemed to like to listen. She talked a lot about Boston. It was her first love after all. They also talked about the ranch, and she asked him questions about his life growing up.

When they finished, he stood and pushed his chair back heavily. "I get up at five. We should go to bed."

Bed?

His eyes had turned to smolder. Slowly, she stood as well.

"Okay."

"Jo, listen - I've never had a woman in my bed who didn't want to be there," he began. "But it's been a long time. So, I am hoping you will join me in it tonight." With that, he stepped around the table and walked past her. She listened to the echo of his boots as he went upstairs.

She felt rooted in place for several seconds, twisting her dinner napkin back and forth in her hands. The attraction she felt toward him was undeniable. And even hours later, she could still remember the taste of his lips on hers. A slight tremor went through her at the memory. It had been a long time for her as well. And he was her husband...

He was sitting on the bed in the first bedroom. There was a large bay window to the left with a window seat. The setting sun painted the room a dusty rose color.

"I don't sleep in the master bedroom," he explained. He watched her as she scanned the bedroom, taking it all in.

"Why?" she asked softly.

"It's not mine. Never was, and I don't see how it could ever be. Is that a problem?"

She shook her head no. She was still standing in the doorway, and they watched each other across the room. She could see his chest rise and fall with each breath. He seemed to be tracing her whole body with his eyes.

"Come to bed," he told her. His voice was a husky whisper.

Again, a tremor went through her. She felt an ache and longing deep inside. She had not just been alone; she had been lonely. And she had been that way long before Nick got arrested.

"Colt." She came to him, straddling his waist and pushing him down on the bed. She leaned over, creating a canopy with her hair. It blocked out the world, so all that was left was the two of them. They held on to each other. Some moments thrashing against the night and all the loneliness that had held them captive. They were iron and lace, colliding in moments of raw, insatiable need. And in other moments, they were soft and gentle and warm like a summer breeze. Their bodies lifting and swaying like waves to the shore.

PART TWO

Joelle rolled over in bed, pulling the covers around her. She opened her eyes to see that the sun was making its way across the sky. She sighed happily. Her whole body felt sated and relaxed. She smiled, thinking of the night before. She could feel her insides vibrate and stir. She wasn't sure any man had ever made her feel that way. She was literally humming from the inside out. She was more than satisfied, yet the hunger for him lingered.

"Jo."

She jumped slightly, then turned back over in bed. Colt was standing over her, completely dressed. He was clean shaven and he smelled wonderful. She reached out, her hand caressing his.

"Come back to bed," she told him.

"Back to bed?" he repeated. "You need to get up."

She blinked and sat up. She wasn't dressed, so she pulled the sheet up around her.

"What's wrong?"

"There's no breakfast made. And I am heading out. There is housework to be done. I thought we discussed all this."

"Colt..."

"I need a partner, Jo."

"I know that." She blinked several more times, pushing back tears that suddenly burned her eyes. "We were partners last night," she said softly.

"I have to start my day. I'll eat some biscuits left over from last night. But I'll be back at noon, and I'd like something hot waiting for me." He turned then and stalked out of the bedroom.

She smacks away a few tears that had managed to escape. She got out of bed, pulling the sheet along with her. She needed a shower and she needed coffee. And she needed to get herself in check. She couldn't lay in bed daydreaming about him all day. He was a business decision, nothing more.

She padded down the hall, the floor cold against her bare feet. Her clothes were still in her suitcase which she'd left in the foyer. The house was silent as she made her way carefully down the winding staircase. Just as she reached the landing, the front door swung open.

A man stood there looking like John Wayne come back to life. He was most likely in his forties. But a life working under the sun had leathered his skin, and it made him appear older.

"Well, I beg your pardon," he said. He respectfully glanced away as she clutched the sheet tighter.

"Who are you?" she asked.

"Jeff Loggings, darling," he said. "You must be Joelle."

"Good morning." Minnie came through the door but stopped in her tracks when she saw Joelle. "Goodness, Jeff." She slapped his arm. "We're sorry to barge in, honey. Go on up and get yourself ready. It looks like you had a wonderful wedding night." She gave Joelle a wink, and then pushed Jeff toward the kitchen.

She grabbed her suitcase and ran back up the stairs. She was out of the shower and dressed in ten minutes. As she headed back downstairs, the smell of perked coffee wafting up to her.

"I hope you don't mind, I got things started," Jeff said, nodding toward the coffee pot.

"Not at all. Thank you." He handed her a steaming cup. Minnie was bustling around, going back and forth between the refrigerator and the pantry.

"How are you settling in?" Jeff asked as they sat down at the table.

"Just fine."

"Is that so?" Jeff gave her a look that remaindered her of her father.

"I slept in," she admitted. She glanced at the clock hanging on the wall. It was a quarter after seven.

"Getting up at dawn takes getting used to. You'll get into the swing of it. Minnie, Colt and I have been doing it our whole lives. I wouldn't know how to sleep in even if I could."

"I could teach you," she said with a smile.

He returned it. "Don't let him scare you off," he said a moment later.

"Scare me off?"

"Colt is certainly rough around the edges. But beneath all that there is a heart of gold. He's just been lonely too long. And he feels the weight of the world on his shoulders. When his daddy died, it about did him in. That was all the family he had, and he was just here one day and gone the next. I don't think Colt even realizes how much it affected him. How much it broke his heart."

She took a long sip from her cup. She certainly knew about heartbreak.

"He doesn't scare me a bit," she said. "I'm quite fond of him." She was surprised to hear some truth in her words.

Jeff leaned across the table and said quietly, "I know how you met. Minnie doesn't. God don't tell her! But I know. And I know Colt told you he wasn't looking for love."

"He did. I'm not looking for love either," she confessed.

"Is that so? Now, darling, everyone is looking for love. Surely, you know that."

"I've had love."

"And how did that work out?"

"Lousy," she replied. "So lousy that it turned me off to the prospect altogether."

Jeff laughed. He had a genuine twinkle in his eye. "If I had a nickel for every time someone said those words. For every time I said those words."

"But aren't you and Minnie married?" she asked.

"Yes. Third time for me, though. I was pretty bitter on love, but there it was all these years – right in front of my face." He stood up then, draining the last of his coffee.

"Minnie, I am heading out," he called. She was just coming out of the pantry. She came over and kissed his cheek. "It was nice meeting you, Jo."

"It was very nice to meet you, too," she told him.

"I'll see you soon." He put on his hat and tipped it toward her. Then he headed out the back door.

***

Minnie stayed for a few hours. She started a pot of chili, and she showed her around the house. It was almost noon when she left, promising to be back the next day. Joelle started a load of laundry and put some cornbread in the oven. It was ready twenty minutes later when Colt came in.

"Smells good," he said.

"Wash up," she told him.

She gave her a tired smile, and memories of the night before flooded her again. She felt her cheeks go warm and her body go flush as he brushed past her. He stood at the kitchen sink for several minutes, washing away the morning. When he finally sat back down, she placed a hot bowl of chili in front of him.

"I have to go into town this afternoon," he said. He turned to his chili and downed half the bowl in a matter of seconds.

"Should I come?" she asked.

"No need. I have an appointment at the bank. I'm a little behind on the mortgage."

She looked up at him. "What do you mean?"

"My daddy was a great man, but his finances were a mess when he died. I've been working day and night to get things in order again. But times are hard."

She dropped her spoon into her bowl. Bits of chili splashed across the table. "I don't understand. I thought you owned this ranch."

"The bank owns the ranch, Jo."

"But you said you could take care of a wife." She didn't know why she suddenly felt so panicky, but she did.

"I can. The manager is a buddy of mine. Everything will be alright," he said. "I'm doing my best. I've been running uphill for three years now."

"I don't know what to say." And she didn't.

"Listen, I apologize if what I said made you believe I owned this ranch right out. I don't. But I hope to someday. I can tell you this, I will always take care of you. But this isn't a prison, it's a marriage. You can leave anytime you want if this isn't what you want."

"Do you want me to leave?"

"No – I don't."

"I just – I can't go back." Tears burned her eyes. She couldn't look up at him. But she heard him push his chair back and come around the table.

"Then don't." He reached down and tilted her head back so she was looking at him. Then he bent and kissed her lips, softly at first and then harder. He pulled her up from the chair and against him. She wanted him. Wanted him right then and there.

As if reading her mind, he lifted her up and onto the table. He came down on top of her, the weight of him making her whole body ache with want. She arched into him and he moaned softly, his breath warm against her ear. And when he took her, she clung to him as if she was lost at sea and he was the only thing keeping her from drowning completely.

***

Colt left the bank feeling uneasy. He was almost three months behind on the mortgage. Not to mention the taxes were due. He had one month to catch up on payments or the ranch will be put up for auction. He hadn't a clue how he would manage, but he was certainly going to try. He just had to work harder. He knew how to do that.

He spent the next few weeks doing just that and showing Joelle the ins and outs of ranch life. She was able to help with some of the manual labor, but not much. He was simply stronger and had been doing it his whole life. There was always hay to cut, bale and stack. Always a fence that needed mending or manure to haul. Joelle helped with other things. She worked a lot in the garden and with the animals. She seemed to enjoy the animals more than anything, especially the horses. He liked watching her with them. In fact, over the next few days, he caught himself watching her more and more.

He also liked coming home to her – most days. It had become painfully obvious she had never kept house before. She could cook - sure, but nothing from scratch. And she tried baking but burned practically everything. She told him that she cleaned every day. He was sure she did. But it was more like tidying up here and there. She had yet to give the whole ranch the good scrubbing that it needed. It was gnawing at him. They had fought about it more than once.

"I just don't know what you want from me!" she told him.

"You know exactly what I want, Jo. Come on."

"A housemaid."

"A partner! Don't act like I don't work myself into an early grave. Is it so much to ask to have a clean house and a decent dinner?"

She stormed out of the room. He found her an hour later, listening to music in the living room. It was a slow song, something country and twangy. The sun had gone down, and the living room was in shadows. He held out his hand to her, and she took it. They swayed together to the music.

"I am trying," she said sadly.

"I know." He held her, getting lost in the moment.

They went upstairs a little later. This is what he longed for all day. It didn't matter if they had bickered all day, he couldn't wait to get under the blankets with her each night. She was beautiful and soft. She awakened things in him that had been dormant for too long. In those moments, he could care less if she knew how to bake bread or use a vacuum. He was completely under her spell.

***

Joelle sat drinking her third cup of coffee. It was late in the day. Colt would be home soon. A part of her hummed with the anticipation of seeing him. The other part of her worried. She glanced around the kitchen and dining room, searching for some spot she hadn't dusted or dish she hadn't washed. She knew he was disappointed. She was not a housewife. At least not one that lived up to his standards. But she was trying. She was becoming more and more aware of how hard she was trying. How much she wanted to make him happy. That made her nervous. There were days when all she thought about was the moment he would walk through the door.

"Hey," he came in just then. He looked rugged and handsome, tired from a long day. "Something smells sweet."

"I baked a cheesecake today," she said proudly. "And I didn't burn it."

"I didn't know you had to actually bake a cheesecake."

"Exactly," she replied. They both smiled.

He sat down, mail in his hand. He began to shuffle through it as she got up to make him a sandwich.

"Jo, why would a lawyer be writing to you?" he questioned.

She stopped mid-step and turned back toward him. "What?"

He held up one of the envelopes and gave her a questioning stare. "Well?"

"I don't know," she said. "Let me have it." She snatched it from her hand.

"What's going on?" he asked with a frown.

"I think it's just about some property I use to own," she lied.

He stood up and came toward her. "Then let's open it." His voice had gone cold.

"It's personal."

"You're my wife..."

"Colt, please."

"Is this about us, Joelle? What are you trying to do – what are you after?"

"After?" she repeated. "What does that mean?"

"Just open the envelope!"

"You think I trying to take something from you? After the past four weeks, that's what you think of me?"

"I don't know what to think. Just open it."

She threw the letter at him, hot tears springing up in her eyes. "This has nothing to do with you. It's about me. I was married before, Colt. He was a drunk and an abuser, and he's in prison now. And now you know."

He took a step back as if he'd been punched in the gut. "You were married before?"

"I was. He took everything I had. He gambled it away. He drank it away. He became violet when it all ran out. And he almost killed someone." Tears were streaming down her cheeks now. "I'm sorry I didn't tell you. I should have."

"Then, why didn't you?"

"A lot of reasons. Mostly because I didn't want you to know. I didn't think you'd want me if you knew, and I needed you to want me. And I was embarrassed. I had been such a fool for him. And it's hard to admit our mistakes sometimes…"

"You lied to me."

"I'm sorry."

"So am I." He turned and walked out the back door.

"Colt," she said. The tears were raging now. She sunk down on the kitchen tile and cried her eyes out.

PART THREE

Colt didn't sleep at all that night. He stayed downstairs on the couch. He could hear Jo above him, pacing the floor. He could hear when she cried. He wanted to go to her, but he couldn't. Finally, he got up and got in the shower. Joelle had finally fallen asleep, and he didn't wake her before he left. He drove into town. Ashlyn was coming to meet him.

He sat at a back table of the local diner. He and Ashlyn had come here almost every weekend when they were dating. He thought about how young and free they had been. He was still young, but he didn't feel very free anymore.

"Colt."

He looked up, and there she was. She looked just the same, if not more beautiful. He stood up as she fluttered into his arms. When they sat down, she reached across the table and held his hand.

"I've missed you," she said. "I heard you got married."

"I did," he replied with a sad smile.

"I'm happy for you. I mean that," she told him.

He nodded slowly. "I know you do."

"Do you love her?" she asked.

Did he?

He knew he had been falling for her more every day. It hadn't been his plan. But it had happened just the same.

"Love is hard," he said.

"It's not," she replied. "Not everyone runs from love, Colt. Not everyone is as big a fool as I am." She squeezed his hand and then let it go. She shuffled around in her purse and then pulled out an envelope. She slid it across the table.

"This should take care of things," she told him.

"I'll pay you back, I swear."

"I know," she said softly. "I am just glad I could help. I love that ranch. And your daddy would be real proud of you."

"Would he?"

"Believe me, he would. You've built a nice life for yourself. You should let yourself enjoy it."

He smiled at her across the table. "Maybe you're right. It meant a lot to see you, but I should go." He stood up, sliding the envelope into his pocket. He came to the table, bent down and kissed the top of her head. "Thank you."

She nodded, reaching up and taking his hand one more time. She held it for a moment and then let him go for good.

***

Colt had been gone all day. It was getting late, and Joelle was drained. She had packed a bag, and she planned on leaving in the morning. Her heart restricted at the thought. Despite her best efforts, she was falling for him. But the truth was out now, and he didn't want her anymore.

"Hi." Colt appeared in the doorway. "I want you to take a ride with me."

She didn't question him. She just got up and followed him outside. It was cold, and she shivered slightly. The world was dark, not even the moon was out as they headed for the barn. One of the horses was out, already saddled.

They rode for a long time without speaking. She felt like they were the only people left in the world. And when they reached a meadow, he got down off the horse and brought her with him. They sunk down in the cool grass, under the sable sky and made love. It was slow and sweet and tender. So much so that she felt like her heart might burst.

"Every day for the past month I have asked myself the same two questions," he said, lying beside her.

"And what are they?" she asked.

"What am I doing? What are we doing?"

"Come up with any answers?"

He gave her a sideways smile. "Some. But they terrify me."

"Why?"

"Because I'm falling in love with you. I broke my promise. And you lied."

"I'm sorry."

"I know. And I know why you did it. You deserve better than him. And I'm sorry for what he did to you." He reached over and took her hand.

"I didn't want to fall for you either. But I did. A little more every day. Colt – please understand. I didn't know how kind a man could be. And yes, you want things your way. You're stubborn and a perfectionist. And you work too hard. But you're also loving and compassionate. Strong and supportive." She turned to face him.

"Jo..."

"I fell for you, too." She had come here to escape love. But everything catches up to you eventually. No point is running. And she supposed she always knew deep down it would be a losing battle. The first time she saw him, she knew. The first time he kissed her, she knew. And when they made love...well, she certainly knew then.

"I promise never to keep anything from you again," she said.

"And I promise to take care of you every day of my life."

"And I promise to love you, Colt. And never leave you."

"I promise to love you and worship you." He kissed her softly. "This time, I'll keep my promises."

She smiled against his lips. "So will I."

THE END

# MY AMISH HOME

## SARAH HAMPTON

It was cold for a mid-June morning. Anna stood by the county road unaffected by the cool breeze. After all, she was used to the hard winters that Seymour could bring. Despite the sun barely rising, the fields were already chirping and buzzing with life. Life started early in the countryside. Anna fidgeted with her luggage. She was not used to doing nothing during the time of day meant for *work*. However, her cousin picking her up had balked at the idea of doing anything before 8 AM, so here she stood and waited on a Friday morning.

She didn't mind waiting. In fact, she was trying to soak in all facets of her familiar home while she could. It was hard to believe that she would be hundreds of miles away by tonight. *Hundreds of miles.* Whisked away by some sort of electric transportation to a new land. Anna had never ridden in a car before. In her opinion, they made far too little noise and could not be trusted. Still, there had to be a reason for Rumspringa to be a time-honored tradition, right? She had heard of girls who never came back. She didn't understand how anyone could turn on their origins. Her parents had told her they would understand whatever she chose to do, but it seemed clear to Anna that they would prefer she stay. After all, they were getting older. She frequently worried about her father working in the field with his bad back. She had always helped him with his work despite her mother's insistence she learn to do "ladylike" crafts instead. As a kid, she would insist on going to the field with her father and carry his tools around, which did not help whatsoever. When she got older, she proved she could work as long and hard as her brothers. Her mother didn't chide her as often now, but she never gave up offering opportunities. *Wouldn't you like to help me cook for this week's market? I could use some help with this quilt. Oh Anna, don't wipe mud on your dress.* She smiled as she thought of her parents. She would be there for them as soon as she returned. She wouldn't allow herself to be dazzled by city lights and electric buggies.

Speaking of which, her electric buggy was supposed to be here by now.

"Where are you, Brittany?" she mumbled absentmindedly as she tapped her wrist.

There was nothing there, of course. She and her friends had seen English people at the markets angrily tapping their digital watches as they demanded punctuality. This had quickly caught on with the children, and it was now the standard among her friends to sarcastically tap their wrists when informing another person of their lateness. Some Amish did wear purely mechanical watches, but it was fairly rare among their order.

She wouldn't see her friends for quite some time. She sat down on her luggage case as she thought about their gathering last night. She was the only one leaving today. The others were either too young or had already returned from their Rumspringas. So, of course, it was an endless torrent of questions and advice. As the night passed, discussion turned to how things would go for Anna.

"I bet Anna will find some rich prince and he'll whisk her away to his foreign castle," giggled her friend Collette.

"Oh, I would never do that," replied Anna, trying to hide a smile.

Collette followed up, unabashed. "Uh huh. And when you do, do you think he'll let us come visit you?"

"Actually," intoned Catherine, "Anna is far too focused on her studies for that sort of thing. If she doesn't watch out, she'll die an old maid."

Anna laughed, but recognized some truth to the statement. "And is that such a bad thing? It seems like wealthy, foreign princes are often in need of old maids. So, I'll still be in a castle."

Collette pounced on this wording, just like Anna knew she would. "Oh, so you admit you're looking for a prince? My, my. I wonder what Elijah would say to that?"

Elijah Beiler was Anna's neighbor and longtime friend. As children, they had quickly struck up a solid friendship due to their mutual hobbies of playing in mud and climbing trees. He was her partner in crime for every dirty, *boyish* activity her friends didn't want to do. They had remained close as they entered their teens. As one could imagine, this spawned lots of teasing and rumors among Anna's girlfriends, but she never allowed herself to take them seriously. If Elijah had any romantic feelings towards her, wouldn't he have shown them by now? After all, frog catching was hardly the courtship material of fantasy novels.

Anna tried to remain deadpan, but couldn't hide the slightest twinge of annoyance in her voice. "I imagine if he had anything to say about it at all, he would had stayed around longer tonight."

She knew it was unfair to blame him for leaving early. He had to help his father pack for the market tomorrow. Still, the petty side of her felt a little disappointed. It was quite likely this would be the last time they would see each other in a long time. Couldn't he sacrifice a little bit of sleep to stay around longer? Truthfully, her feelings for him had changed over time. As they developed into adults, she had come to view him in a way she didn't think he reciprocated. Her friends never gave up an opportunity to tease her about his boyish good looks, his olive skin, or his muscular, strong body built from working the farm since he could hold a hoe. No one ever believed her, but she didn't really care about that. She liked him because of how close they were. She had shared a lot with him and he always accepted her the way she was. In addition, though Elijah was not a purposefully funny man, he always made her laugh with his deadpan, straightforward statements. Anna had trouble imagining developing the same level of bond with another person, let alone another man. Besides, who else would want a girl who wipes mud on her dresses?

Anna stopped her thoughts there. She was supposed to be annoyed at him. The sun was fully shining now. A few strands of her dark red hair obstructed her view. She blew at them forcefully like they somehow represented Elijah. They fluttered a little bit and fell back. She blew at them again—harder this time.

"You know, if you keep doing that, you'll feel lightheaded."

Anna was never one to scream, but the sudden male voice made her jump. She turned around to see Elijah climbing over the fence on the side of the road toward her. She briefly felt a moment of panic about the thoughts she had been having. She knew she had an occasional habit of thinking out loud. If Elijah had heard anything, it didn't show on his face. He walked up to her, took off his hat, and ran his hand through his dark hair while he eyed her worriedly.

"Are you okay? Your face is a little red. It could be the oxygen deprivation."

Anna quickly composed herself. "Eli. My face is perfectly fine, thank you very much. What are you doing here?"

She looked behind him. There were only cows munching grass in the field. "How did you even get here anyway?"

Elijah blinked. "I walked."

"From the market? That must have been five miles."

"I wanted to see you off."

Anna was pleasantly surprised but didn't let it show. "Why didn't you see me off last night then, like everyone else?" she snapped. "And what about your father's market stall?"

Elijah was unfazed. "It was a slow day and I asked if I could leave early. And, well, you seemed to be enjoying time with your friends last night and we wouldn't have had time to talk."

This was an unexpectedly soft sentiment from Elijah, and Anna couldn't think of a quick response.

"I'm just glad I caught you before you left," he added.

Anna tried to hold on to her annoyance. "Well, you almost didn't. I should be gone by now."

"With Brittany picking you up? You'd be lucky if she's awake by now." He rubbed his right leg distractedly. "Plus, I angered a few cows and had to take an unexpected detour."

At this, Anna had to laugh. She stepped forward to embrace him and they sat and made small talk for a few passing minutes. Something popped into her mind.

"So, what did you want to talk to me about last night?

She could see him visibly tense and his countenance changed. There was a small pause before he answered.

"It's just that you're leaving, and I won't see you for a while..." His speaking patterns were too slow and steady for stuttering, but Anna could sense indecision whirring in his brain.

"Yes. And?"

Elijah continued, "I thought I should tell you..." He paused to think. "That you shouldn't..."

Anna was thoroughly confused. "I shouldn't leave? I shouldn't talk to strangers? I shouldn't learn to dance the can-can?"

Elijah was stone-faced but Anna could sense an inner sigh. Whatever he wanted to say, he wouldn't be saying it today.

"You shouldn't forget to say your morning prayers, that's all." He stood and looked down the road. "It seems as if your cousin does have some work ethic. I believe I hear her car."

With that, he gave a goodbye hug and went on his way. Anna couldn't see a car in the distance, but Elijah always had weirdly good hearing. And she couldn't, for the life of her, think of what he possibly wanted to tell her.

—-

Sure enough, after a short while, Anna could hear the familiar sound of Brittany's red Toyota Camry traveling down the dirt road at breakneck speeds. When it arrived, Anna jumped back and let out an exasperated huff. The window rolled down to reveal her ecstatic cousin, designer sunglasses placed on her perfectly styled brunette hair to show her green eyes twinkling with excitement.

"Do all English people drive like that?" cried Anna.

Brittany laughed, "I'm the best driver in Chicago! You haven't seen the half of it."

Anna sighed. "At this rate, I fear I won't even make it to the city."

Brittany winked and got out to help Anna with her luggage. "Don't be such a worrywart! Trust me. You are in great hands."

She stopped to wave at Anna's family approaching behind her. They had heard the car too and were coming to say goodbye. "Now, hurry up and get in! We have a schedule to keep, you know."

Anna's littlest brother Jakob, with the energy only bestowed upon the quite young, was the first to arrive. He came to a sudden stop upon closer look at the strange large machine of transportation. The look of awe on her brother's face made Anna giggle. She remembered the first time she had seen an "electric buggy".

"Jakob! Don't even think about climbing on that car!" shouted Anna's mother, Abigail.

"But, how else am I going to ride it?" asked the confused 6-year old.

"I'll explain it to you later, son. Get back now. It's time for Anna to go."

The young boy frowned, stepped back, and asked with sadness, "You'll come back soon, right Anna?"

Anna picked him up and held him tightly. "Of course I will. I'll have presents for you too!"

At the talk of presents, Jakob immediately perked up and was back to his cheerful self again. Abigail smiled as each of Anna's siblings said their goodbyes. Her father approached and handed her a small parcel. She looked inside. It was a blue and white quilt she had made when she was 11 years old.

"It might get chilly in Chicago. You wouldn't want to catch a cold." Her father said gently.

Anna smiled gratefully and touched her father's hand. "I'll bring it back with me soon."

—-

The drive to Chicago seemed to go by quickly as she and Brittany caught each other up on their lives. They made several stops along the way, as Brittany saw things that caught her fancy. Soon after they arrived in the city, discussion came to Anna's new job.

"So, basically you'll just assist with office work. You'll organize files, help with scheduling, and basically anything else Dr. Jamison wants." Brittany explained in her trademark fast pace, no wear in her voice even after hours of nonstop talking.

Anna nodded, "Is that what you do?"

Brittany laughed. "No. I don't even technically work there. My firm handles their marketing campaigns. You'll love your coworkers though. They're good friends of mine. You'll like Dr. Jamison too, and maybe his son."

Anna nodded again, mesmerized by the electric glow of the world passing by outside. The sun was beginning to set and the city's neon lights grew brighter in comparison. By the time they arrived at Brittany's condo, the night had completely settled. Anna was feeling exhausted from the ride, but Brittany didn't show any signs of stopping as she unlocked and opened the door.

"Ta da! I didn't have a chance to get a key copied for you, so we'll have to do that tomorrow. Oh, there's the cutest coffeeshop down the street from the locksmith. I've been meaning to try it. We can go there together! Of course, first we'll have to get you some new clothes at the shopping mall."

Anna yawned and sat down. "The shopping mall?"

Brittany gave Anna a bemused look. She knew the Amish knew more about outside life than most people thought. She was always careful not to be condescending. "It's like... A big farmer's market." Brittany said slowly.

Anna laughed, "I know what a shopping mall is. I already have clothes though."

This remark got an alarmed look from Brittany. "Oh, but you don't plan on wearing those out here do you?"

"Well, yes I did."

Brittany spirits looked visibly doused. "Well, okay. I'm sure the clinic has a dress code, though, so we should still get you some office clothing..."

Anna relented a bit. "Oh yes. But afterwards, perhaps we could go shopping for some fun modern styles? You know how clueless I am towards fashion."

Brittany's face lit up instantly, "That would be great! It'll be so much fun. In fact, I may know a mall that's still open now..." She said, already checking her smartphone for opening hours.

"Actually," Anna said quickly, giving a more exaggerated yawn this time, "I'm feeling pretty tired. Do you mind if we just stay here tonight?"

And so they did. Brittany made a pasta dinner for the two of them using packaged foods Anna had never seen. They spent the rest of the night watching old movies. Anna concluded her first night in the city falling asleep on the couch, not as enthused by the technological marvel of television as Brittany had hoped.

—-

The rest of the weekend passed in what seemed like a whirlwind to Anna. There seemed to be no end to the amount of things Brittany wanted to show Anna. They had been friends since they were very young, and got along effortlessly. The city girl took Anna shopping for clothes first, of course. After hours of trying on dresses, tops, bottoms, accessories, and what seemed like every shoe in the store, they finally found a wardrobe that was chic enough for Brittany and sensible enough for Anna.

Anna found that her cousin's energetic nature was infectious, and soon was genuinely excited to do the many things suggested to her. Naturally, this delighted Brittany. More hours were spent meeting her friends and Anna's new coworkers. They seemed to truly be interested in Anna's stories of her Amish life and her observations of the city. During mealtimes, Brittany seemed to insist Anna try a new style of food every time. Anna preferred her mother's cooking, but still marveled at the variety available.

Sunday night, Brittany handed Anna a brand-new smartphone and explained how to use it. She had already added the number for her phone, emergency services, and local restaurants to the contacts. She had also created a Facebook account for Anna. The account had 7 "friends," which Anna imagined to be a lot. Brittany then gave Anna her credit card with Anna's name on it.

When Anna protested, Brittany waved it off and said "I don't have any siblings and I don't plan to have children any time soon. I make more money than I need. I don't have anyone else to care for, and you're like a little sister to me. I leave town pretty frequently, so I want you to be covered. Just in case."

Anna kept the card in her new wallet but told herself she would only use it in emergencies.

—-

Compared to the pace of the weekend, her office job seemed to be in slow-motion. She had carried a few boxes and retrieved a few files, but a large part of her time was spent sitting in a comfortable leather chair. Accustomed to the hard labor of working her family's farm, Anna kept asking if there was more work to be done.

Her coworkers found this funny. "You are working. You're sitting there, smiling at patients who come in, and telling them where to sit. This business would fall apart without you. You are the backbone of this operation, not Dr. Jamison," they said. Overhearing this comment, Dr. Jamison laughed and assured Anna she was doing perfectly fine.

The bell dinged and a tall, well-dressed young man with neatly groomed blond hair entered.

"Hello!" enthused Anna. "Please have a seat. Do you have an appointment with Dr. Jamison?"

The young man gave Anna a smile. "I am Dr. Jamison."

"Not yet you're not," her boss's voice interjected before Anna could react. "Your board results haven't come in yet."

The young man approached Anna's desk so he could more clearly see Dr. Jamison behind her. "Yes, father. I'm aware of that. I'm sure I know what the results are, though. Are you thinking I could have failed?" Now that he was closer, Anna could detect a hint of cologne. The subtly pleasant scent contrasted with the edge in his words.

Dr. Jamison, who had been very open and friendly to Anna, didn't even look up from his paperwork and spoke with an admonishing tone which she sensed was very familiar to this young man. "Yes, Christopher. There is always a chance. One day you'll see beyond your ego and realize that."

The young man took a step back and gave a light shrug at Anna. "Very well. Not Dr. Jamison, then. Just Chris, for the moment. I came to drop off a few documents for the *doctor*. I need to speak with him about them."

"Not now, Christopher. I have to prepare these files and then I have patients. Come back at 4:30," came the reply.

To this, the young man gave a thin smile and left without another word, leaving Dr. Jamison shaking his head. Anna offered no comment, but was surprised at how tense English families could be.

—-

At 5 PM came closing time. Again, it surprised Anna to end the workday so long before sun down. Her new coworkers said their goodbyes, already treating her like they were the oldest of friends. Anna sat and waited on the outside deck for Brittany's car. She was a bit late, but that was not uncommon. A true sign of a newcomer to the city, Anna spent the time looking at the cityscape and passing cars instead of playing on her phone.

About fifteen minutes later, Chris showed up looking for his father. Approaching the building, he could see the lights in the office were already dark and sighed. He walked up to the door, not seeming to notice Anna.

She spoke up. "Oh, I think he's already gone. I'm sorry."

She almost instantly regretted saying anything. Based on her previous interaction with this young man, she expected him to offer a snide comment or disparaging look. However, he just sighed again and sat down in a chair across from her.

"I figured he would be. He knows I have lessons until 5. Lunchtime is the only time we were both supposed to be free." He ran his thin fingers through his hair, partially ruining the perfect streaks.

"Why did he tell you to come back at 4:30 then, if he knows you can't make it?"

Chris massaged his temples. "It's his way of saying he's too busy for me."

Anna was surprised to see a vulnerable side to what she had originally perceived as a highly-strung, egotistical man. Having nothing else to do, she decided to probe further.

"Isn't he proud of you, though? You're going to be a doctor." She hesitated before adding the next part but went ahead. "You don't even look old enough to be one."

The young man looked up at Anna. For a moment, she feared she had angered him but he simply laughed and said "I'm sorry, what is your name again? I suppose I've already offered you mine."

Anna offered out her hand, "I'm Anna. I'm new here."

Chris shook her hand. "Chris Jamison. I can tell you're new." His hands were pale but surprisingly warm.

Anna giggled and he continued, "To answer your question, I graduated from university early and went to medical school afterwards. The medical board also thought I was too young, but agreed to allow me to take the examinations, provided I don't practice until next year."

"Next year?"

"When I turn eighteen."

This confused Anna. "So that means you're only..."

"Seventeen, yes. I get these questions a lot."

Chris was only one year older that she was. She took in his facial structure again. He was older than he looked, then. She probed further. "So you're pretty smart, huh?"

This prompted a laugh. "Some might say so. Others, not so much. In truth, I've just always been a very curious person. I read a lot of books as a child."

This seemed unexpectedly modest to Anna from a man characterized as egotistical by his own father. She felt some admiration for what he had achieved at such a young age. "Wow," she mumbled, thinking about her own life.

He leaned back in his chair, his previous melancholy mood forgotten. "So did my father hire you to guard his door? You look a bit too nice for that."

Anna checked the time on her new phone. "Well, I'm waiting for my cousin to come pick me up, but she's late and she hasn't called."

Chris leaned over a little to look at her phone. "Has she texted? You have an unread message."

"Has she what? Oh!" Anna had forgotten about this feature on her phone. She pulled up her messages, and sure enough, she saw one from Brittany.

*Hi Anna!!! How was your first day at work? I can't wait to hear about it. My meeting got delayed and I won't be able to get free for several hours! Sorry. Go out with Mike and Kelly. I'll call you when I'm done! XOXOXO"*

This message was interspersed with curious yellow cartoon faces, which Anna took to represent exaggerated emotions. Mike and Kelly were her new coworkers. She looked up at their parking spaces. Empty.

Chris took in the look on her face. "It seems that she won't be here for a while."

Anna got up. "Yeah, she's in a meeting. It's okay. I can walk home."

At this, Chris laughed and shook his head.

"What?" said Anna, defensively.

"No offense, but that would be like a puppy walking in the Amazon. You look curious and trusting. That's a dead giveaway you're new to the city. A perfect target for predators."

The last word brought images of bears and wolves to Anna's mind, but then she understood what he meant.

He pressed on, "Plus, I'm willing to bet you're not quite sure how to get home anyway."

That was true. Anna hesitated. "Well..."

Chis stood up and started walking down the front steps. "Come on, I'll drive you."

Anna stood still. "What?"

Christ kept walking. "I'll drive you. You don't want to take a taxi. They charge double rates to people who look like tourists, which you do. My father clearly isn't here, so I have some free time."

Anna followed him a little bit so she could hear what he was saying. She didn't want to be impolite. However, she wasn't sure if she could trust this complicated young man. As Chris opened the driver door to his sleek black Mercedes, he turned to look at her.

"Come on. You can tell your cousin what you're doing. You'll be perfectly safe."

*That's right*, Anna thought. *Didn't Brittany say she knew Dr. Jamison's son?* She looked up at the sky. It was cloudy, as it often was in

Chicago. She didn't particularly feel like being caught in the rain. She shrugged internally and ran towards Chris's car. *In the spirit of running around, right?*

—-

Not long after they began driving, drops of rain started to appear on the windshield. Anna breathed an internal sigh of relief. Although she didn't think she displayed any outward emotion, Chris seemed to know what she was thinking and gave her a smile.

"Where do you live again?" Chris asked, pulling up the GPS on his dashboard.

*I guess it would be silly to hide that now*, Anna thought. "In the 600 North Fairbanks Condos. Have you been there?"

"No, but soon I will," he said, typing in the address with soft, precise touches.

Anna watched him. "You know, I wouldn't know personally, but I've heard it's bad to text and drive."

Chris looked and her and shrugged. "You do it, then."

Anna looked over at the glowing screen on his dashboard. After some trouble, she managed to get the device to do what she wanted. She looked over at Chris, quite pleased with herself.

Chris gave a light chuckle but didn't comment. After a short pause, he spoke again. "So how was your first week in English society?"

She was disappointed "I thought I set up the GPS correctly."

"Oh no, you did well. See?" He pointed to the screen where it said her address.

"Then how—" she started.

"Your clothes. It's your first time wearing them. The scent of the clothing shop is still on them. I didn't think you would have chosen that perfume for yourself, it's a bit bold for someone like you. Plus, you've already told me you're from out of town."

He paused to sip water out of a glass bottle before continuing. "It's not just a new outfit for a new job, either. Every time you lean over, you're instinctively rolling up sleeves that aren't there. You're not used to wearing short-sleeve clothing, but your arms are still tan. Very unusual for a city dweller."

Anna felt a little embarrassed, for some reason. "Maybe I'm just from the country," she challenged.

Chris nodded, "Your accent is slightly southern, but you're not used to any sort of machinery. You subconsciously hold your breath when I accelerate quickly. And why would a girl your age move to Chicago to live with her cousin? You're too young for college. I'm guessing you're on your Rumspringa. How is it?"

Anna took this in. "But how did you know it was the first week?"

He laughed. "Because you check your phone very infrequently for a millennial. My father's clinic has had Amish workers before, and that usually changes after the first week."

Anna found his statements to seem somewhat presumptuous, even though they were factual and things she would freely tell people. "It actually hasn't been a week," she huffed.

This tone made Chris glance over at her again. "I'm sorry. That made you uncomfortable, didn't it?" he mused. "Sometimes I get excited and get ahead of myself. Maybe I do need to see past my own ego."

She decided to encourage this softer side of him. "It's okay. It was true."

He responded with a smile and they drove in silence for a while.

A thought occurred to Anna and she spoke up again. "Did you notice anything else?"

This time, he waited before answering. He pointed to a road sign for a bakery. "You're probably hungry," he finally offered.

Anna hadn't eaten since breakfast and she suddenly felt the pangs of hunger. She looked at her new watch. There was plenty of time before Brittany got off work. She agreed to go eat.

"Did you just guess?" she asked.

"Yes," said Chris, pulling into the parking lot. He decided not to tell Anna he had trained himself to guess a person's last meal from the smell of their breath.

—-

Anna thought about Chris and the bakery as she opened the door to Brittany's condo. She had had an unexpectedly good time. The bakery turned out to be owned by Italians. It was undoubtedly Anna's favorite place in the city so far. She expected herself to return soon. She smiled as she remembered the welcoming nature of the middle-aged couple that owned it. They had greeted her and Chris like old friends and seemed genuinely sorry to see them leave. Truthfully, it reminded Anna of how people were in her hometown. Apparently, Chris was a regular customer there.

She had learned a lot about Chris. As they told each other about their lives, they discovered that they shared a surprising amount of interests. They both loved classical art, piano music, and reading. Chris, who had initially come across as cold and standoffish, was an extremely passionate person. As he had said earlier, he was very curious. This applied to virtually everything. He told her about various authors and their differing viewpoints on a broad spectrum of subjects, including astronomy, medicine, philosophy, art, history, theatre, and literature. She didn't understand all of the terminology he used, but as a curious person herself, it was intrinsically interesting. Chris was pleasantly surprised when she brought up her own theories and questions. He was used to people nodding along and feigning interest. Anna appreciated how he answered her questions and explained things simply without seeming condescending.

When she mentioned this, he said "Einstein believed that if a person couldn't explain something simply, then they didn't understand it well enough." This was followed by a quick list of little-known Einstein facts.

They had stayed much later than she had expected, but Brittany had informed her via text that she had stopped to get a few drinks with friends after work anyway. As Anna rested in one of Brittany's brightly-colored lounge chairs, she was surprised to find that the smile on her face was from thoughts of Chris as much as thoughts of the bakery. She thought fondly of his enthusiasm and charm. *Are all men in the city like this?* she wondered.

As she was thinking about taking a shower, Brittany burst into the room. Her cousin changed out of her office clothing in what Anna thought must be record-breaking speed, all the while talking about her day. In less than a minute, Brittany was reclined next to Anna, dressed in evening wear and sipping a glass of Zinfandel.

"Anyway, enough about me. Your first day at work! How was it? I'm sorry I couldn't pick you up. I'm sure you were okay with Mike and Kelly, though. I think they're dating now. But I thought Mike was gay? Maybe he just dresses well. Which one drove you home?"

She paused to take a drink and Anna picked this opportunity to speak before more questions came.

"My first day went really well. And, actually, Chris drove me home." She realized that she had forgotten to tell Brittany with who gave her a ride.

Brittany paused mid-sip. "Chris Jamison?"

"Yes, him."

She looked up at Anna, her eyes bristling with the excitement of possible gossip. "He's cute, isn't he? Tell me everything."

So Anna did, starting from his office visit to the bakery to the ride home. Brittany listened intently, nodding along to every sentence. When Anna finished, her cousin beamed at her.

"Oh, Anna, that's great! I'm so glad my meeting ran late, now! I wonder, would that be divine intervention? I did throw a penny into the fountain at the mall." She scratched her chin.

Anna wrinkled her brow. "What?"

Brittany sat up and looked at Anna. "It sounds like you two hit it off. He clearly likes you."

Anna was still confused. "You mean, romantically?"

"Yes, romantically! He *likes* likes you. He's usually very involved with himself and doesn't talk much to anyone else. You must have caught his eye. I knew buying that blouse was the right decision!" Brittany looked like she was on the verge of squealing.

This seemed doubtful to Anna. "Well, I don't know about that..."

Brittany went into a neutral expression. "Oh, you don't like him?"

Anna hadn't even considered this. She had just met him, after all. *Life moves so fast in the city*, she thought.

"It's not that. I just..." she stopped, not knowing what to say. She had only felt that way about Elijah, before. She thought about the last time she'd seen him. Although it made her stomach clench a bit, she decided to tell Brittany about her feelings for her long-time neighbor and friend. After she was done, she felt as if a weight had been lifted from her chest.

Brittany nodded, taking this in. "I'd wondered if anything was going on between you two."

"Well, there's not. I don't think he feels that way about me and I don't know anything about Chris."

Brittany stood up and stretched, finally seeming to slow down. "Well, go out on a few dates with Chris and see how you like him. You can always stop."

"Go out?"

Brittany turned to look Anna in the eye. "He did ask you out somewhere, right?"

Anna thought about this. "Well, he did mention taking me to the theatre this weekend."

She told Brittany more about it. As she finished, Brittany excitedly spoke. "That's a date!"

"Is it?" Anna said, flabbergasted.

"Yes! We'll have to decide what you wear! Oh, so little time to shop."

As Brittany started talking to herself about outfit possibilities, Anna thought about what she wanted to do. She was unsure about dating anyone, but she found that she was quite excited at the thought of seeing Chris again. *I'll go,* she decided, *and then we'll see what happens.*

—-

The week passed uneventfully except for the weather cooling unexpectedly. The condo was well heated, but it made Anna feel a little warmer on the inside when she slept in the quilt her father gave her. Then, the weekend came and Chris took her to the theatre. The production was *Les Miserables*. She had read the book before, but was awestruck to see the plot re-enacted by the characters' singing voices. The main character, Jean Valjean, was played by a handsome man with a passionate voice. When the story ended, Anna was surprised to find a single tear rolling down her left cheek. Chris, not taking his eyes off the stage, offered her a handkerchief.

As they were leaving the theatre, it was chilly and Chris draped his dark blazer over her shoulders. They talked about the play as they walked back to the car and on the drive back. They shared their favorite parts and he told her about the history involved in the plot. He drove her to the front entrance of the condos and exited the car to open the door for her. He held her gently by the shoulders when she stood up.

"So, what did you think?" he asked.

She didn't think he was talking about the play. "I really had a good time," she replied quietly. She meant it, and offered him a warm smile.

He returned it. "Would you like to go out again next weekend?"

She thought about it. Despite what she discussed with Brittany, she wasn't completely comfortable with courting someone she just met. In her home community, courtships were serious business, and people only began them after knowing the person for some time. However, it seemed that the English use dating as a way of getting to know someone. She really hadn't felt uncomfortable tonight at all. In fact, she was surprised at how relaxed Chris made her.

"Yes," she said, smiling wider. The smile hadn't faded by the time she walked into her condo. Brittany was, of course, ecstatic.

—-

As it turned out, she saw him before that weekend. The following Wednesday, he had come in to see his father after work and they went out for coffee afterwards. There was a Starbucks coffeehouse on the street of her workplace, but Chris had turned his nose up at that. He took her to a hole-in-the-wall place with excellent pastries and beautiful latte art. She had always liked dark coffee, but she found that she was becoming attached to the more ornate espresso drinks popular among English girls.

They still went out that weekend. They went out next weekend too. The following month flew by as they saw each other more frequently. She felt as if he was trying to take her to everywhere in the city. They went hiking, boating, and even jet skiing once. He was teaching her how to drive, and she was doing surprisingly well. He tried to sign her up for a gym, but she just couldn't see why people would pay money to lift heavy objects.

She remembered one time in particular. They had planned to go see an outdoor concert in the evening, but a sudden downpour had caused the band to reschedule. He suggested they go to his house and she agreed. She discovered he lived slightly outside of city limits. They were soon pulling into the driveway of an enormous building on top of a hill.

"What part of this is yours?" she asked, craning her head to see how high the manor went.

He laughed. "All of it. Well, my family technically owns it, but I'm the eldest of two heirs."

He explained that his family members were mostly wealthy businessmen in the pharmaceutical industry. Only he and his father were currently doctors. His family has supported him through medical school, but he wanted to eventually break off and make his own living. This was not a popular decision among his family, and led to tension between him and his father.

Chris opened the front door for Anna and she walked in. She took in the beautiful architecture of the convex ceiling. Chris strolled in to the dimly lit area and pointed to a piano at the far end of the living room. It was illuminated by the light of a large window. Anna could see droplets of the rain sticking to the window, casting wide shadows within the building.

"This is where I've been spending a lot of time since I finished school," he said, sitting down in front of it. He gestured to Anna to sit next to him.

The music he played was dark and haunting at first. Each note, already chilling, rang throughout the spacious chamber, adding to the macabre feeling. Anna shivered, even though she was perfectly warm. The melody soon slowed and became melancholy. The tempo seemed to match that of water droplets slowly dripping off a rooftop after a large storm, adding a mere trickle to the flood that came before. The song transformed once more into a brighter emotion. Anna tried to pinpoint what it was. It wasn't quite happiness. She realized it was *hope*. The song was about hope.

When he finished, she spoke first. "It's beautiful. What is it about?

Chris continued to play an improvisational melody. "Addiction. It's an addict's tale. I was first inspired to write it when I studied the effects of drugs on people in school. It made me start my research into curing addictions."

"I thought you were still taking piano lessons?"

"I am. I'll never be too good to learn."

They didn't say much afterwards. He played music late into the night. Anna listened and watched the raindrops on the windows.

—-

Anna woke up bright and early the next day. She was still dazed from last night. She wasn't quite sure where their relationship was going, but she liked him for sure. She thought about his goodnight kiss last night and wondered if it was a dream. She could still feel the tingle of his warm lips on hers. She could still smell his pleasant scent as he leaned in and put his hand on the side of her face. Surely it wasn't a dream. The kiss was gentle and cautious—sweeter than she would have expected from him. She was smiling absentmindedly as she walked into the kitchen.

"I take it you had a nice time with Dr. Jamison?" Brittany inquired slyly.

Anna made a face. "Don't call him that. I always think of Chris's father instead."

Chris's board results had come in. As he suspected, he did not fail. However, he still had to wait a year before beginning an internship. Anna sat down. "I did have a wonderful time, though. I think I am beginning to like Chris," she blushed.

Brittany laughed. "You'd better get ready because Chris called and asked you to breakfast this morning. It seems he likes you too. "

"Oh, he called you?"

"Well, he tried getting a hold of you... but somebody never answers their phone," Brittany said pointedly as she walked out of the kitchen with her morning smoothie.

Anna dashed for her phone. Sure enough, she saw a couple of messages and a missed call from Chris. She smacked her forehead in exasperation. "Why is it so hard for me to remember this walkie talkie telephone?" she mumbled angrily.

Brittany chuckled and called from the living room. "It'll probably take you some time to get used to. Don't worry! Chris understands. He wasn't upset at all. We just made fun of you for about 10 minutes. "

"At least my struggles are entertaining to you two," Anna deadpanned.

"They are! I'll be thinking about them all day at work. I must get going now. You better get ready. He'll be here in 30 minutes." Brittany was quickly out the door and the ding of the elevator could be heard shortly after. Anna decided to wash up and put on her brand-new navy blue dress. She slipped on her sweater and shoes and almost immediately heard a knock at the door. She swung it open, already elated.

"You have good timing! I just put my shoes on and—"

Anna stopped as she stared into familiar brown eyes. *Chris doesn't have brown eyes,* she thought. Instead, a disheveled, exhausted-looking Elijah stood in the doorway.

Before she could react, he spoke. "Anna I need you to come with me." There was urgency in his voice.

"Elijah! What are you doing here? Is something wrong?"

Elijah spoke quickly, which was unusual for him. "Your father has had an accident. He's been admitted into Mercy Hospital St Louis. Your mother is there with him. The others had to stay home. Your mother asked me to come get you. She says she hears your father say your name at night. His spine is injured badly. They will operate on him soon. We have to hurry."

Anna stood there in shock. Elijah tugging on her hand snapped her back to reality. Unable to process everything, she grabbed her bag and followed Elijah outside. There was a taxi waiting for them.

"What happened, Eli?" she asked as they got in.

Elijah explained while the driver pulled onto the highway. "Our barn was damaged in a storm a few days ago. Some raccoons and coyotes have been trying to get in and attack the livestock. When we had to miss the market, your father came by with your brothers to help us with the repairs. I can't tell you what a godsend their help was. Halfway through, it started storming again. Harder this time. Your father was in the beams when the structure began to collapse. We tried to get to him in time, but the structure fell a few seconds later. Levi was crushed in between the beams. We had to get the lift to pull him out. He was still holding up when they drove him to see Dr. Kimberly, but she sent him to Mercy as his condition worsened. I went with your mother there. They figured it would be faster than mail if I went to get you. So, here I am."

Anna took this in quietly. She was known for being calm in emergencies. "Thank you for caring for my mother, Eli. My family needs our support right now. You were right to get me."

The remainder of the drive was silent until they pulled into an airport parking lot.

"We're flying?" Anna turned to Elijah with a start. It was highly uncommon in their order, but it was allowed during emergencies.

Elijah just grabbed Anna's hand. "Just stay near me. I'll keep you safe. I promise."

Anna nodded as a calm washed over her. She hadn't seen him in a while, but Elijah always meant what he said. She had faith that God had sent him to bring her back.

Elijah took care of checking in and was with her through the entire ordeal. His father had flown once before and had taught him the basics, in case he ever needed it. Anna had little time to process the procedure.

Everything was happening so suddenly; it felt like she wasn't part of reality anymore.

They soon boarded the plane and were on their way to St Louis. Elijah was still holding Anna's hand as they flew. She subconsciously rested her head on his shoulder and soon drifted off to sleep, still tired from last night. Despite the urgency of the situation, she felt at peace flying through the clouds with this man that she'd known since childhood.

As Elijah watched her fall asleep on his arm, he couldn't help but feel content. He leaned back and let the satisfaction and happiness wash over him. He hadn't felt this since Anna left. He hadn't mentioned it, but it was actually his idea to get Anna himself. Her mother had been too distraught to think about much. She had no idea how to reach Anna. After he convinced Abigail that he could bring her back, he was on the next flight to Chicago.

He watched her chest rise and fall as she breathed. *I have to tell her, but not yet,* he thought. She was already going through a lot. He didn't want to overwhelm her. He decided to just enjoy the moment. He looked at the woman he had loved for years. He knew he wanted to be with her anywhere she went. Hand in hand. *I love you, Anna.*

—-

Anna sat in the waiting room as the surgeons worked to save her father. He had been unconscious when they arrived, but she held his hand and spoke with him regardless. She was convinced he could hear her, and her thoughts were confirmed by squeezes from his hand. She had held it until the aides came to take him to his operation. She now looked at a text message from Chris on her phone. She had sent him a hurried message about the situation as they boarded the plane. She looked at his brief response.

*Okay. I'll be there soon.*

*Be there soon?* she wondered. *He's coming to St. Louis?* Sure enough, he showed up 30 minutes after she did. However, he didn't say much. He asked Anna some specifics about her father's condition. She didn't know, so he donned a lab coat and went to speak with the doctors. She could hear the whispers from the hospital staff. Apparently, he was somewhat famous among the medical community for graduating medical school in his teens. *Why couldn't he tell me more about my father? Why can't any of the doctors do that?* She looked over at Elijah, who was finally asleep after three days awake. *Without him, I wouldn't have known for several days.*

The sound of the operating room exit slamming open jolted him awake. Chris, in surgical attire, walked out with a clipboard in a hurried manner.

"Good news. There was a time when we thought he wasn't going to make it, but he somehow rallied and got through the woods. Your father is going to be okay."

He pulled off his mask. "They wouldn't let me touch him, of course. Not enough experience. After some convincing, they allowed me to observe. I've seen cases like this before. He's lucky to be alive. How much he'll recover remains to be seen."

Anna's eyes were wet with joy. Chris moved to sit next to her, but Elijah suddenly jumped up.

"So that's it? Mr. Miller will definitely be okay?"

"Yes. They're finishing up with him right now, but I wanted to come out and tell you." Chris said slowly, with Elijah already furiously pumping his hand in a firm handshake. He rubbed his thin fingers afterwards, wondering who this man was.

Elijah spoke with gratitude. "Thank you very much, doctor. We are forever in your debt."

"Of course. Who—"

Chris was cut off as Elijah moved in front of Anna. "Anna, now that we know your father will be okay, there's something I have to say.

It might not be the best time, but I can't wait any longer. I should have told you the day you were leaving, but I couldn't. I wanted to tell you on the plane, but you had too much on your mind. But I have to tell you now."

And, so he did. He told her that he had loved her for many years now. He talked about the adventures and laughter they had shared from since they were very little. He described the moment he knew he wanted to spend his life with her. He talked about the many times he almost told her his feelings.

"I wanted to tell you sooner. I should have told you sooner, but I was too worried about losing you. But since you've gone, I've felt this burning fire in my gut because you didn't know. It wasn't until then that I realized I had to tell you, regardless of your response."

Anna stood in shocked silence. She was already very emotional from the news about her father. She wondered what Elijah meant by "too much on her mind," as there was still quite a lot. He was usually a man of few words. She must have had these words in his mind for a long time.

He took her hand in his and held it. "And I mean that. I would never pressure you to do something you don't want. To *feel* a way you don't feel. I just wanted you to know, and tomorrow seemed too far away."

Anna stared at him unblinkingly. She felt paralyzed by the hurricane of emotions whirling through her. She wondered if Elijah knew this. She finally managed the strength to glance over at Chris. His face was unreadable, but he set down his clipboard, threw up his hands, and walked out.

"Elijah, I..." she managed.

He patted her hand. "You don't have to say anything right now. Think about it. Or don't. Don't feel obligated to do anything. No matter what happens, I'll love you. I'll love you as a life partner or as a friend, depending on what you need. Just take your time."

With those words, he let go of her hand, put on his hat, and strolled away as if nothing happened.

—-

The next two months were a complex time for Anna. She and her mother were overjoyed at her father's recovery, but he was still bedridden for the foreseeable future. In addition, the steep hospital bills suddenly left the family in debt with the primary breadwinner unable to work. Anna responded to this by taking on a second job at a nearby diner. Days passed by in a blur, but not the kind that comes with fun times. For Anna, this was the blur of sleep deprivation and exhaustion. After a long day at the Jamison clinic, she threw herself into washing dishes and sweeping floors. She often didn't come home until well after midnight, sometimes catching a worried look from Brittany before collapsing on her bed. After a few short hours of sleep, her day would begin again.

Brittany had insisted upon helping with the family bills. Her initial financial support was how the family avoided bankruptcy. However, much of her assets were tied up in physical investments and stocks, and couldn't be quickly liquified. Still, Anna couldn't thank her enough and promised she would repay her. She had already used her previously untouched credit card to make her way back to Chicago.

Anna knew the grind of hard times and took it in stride, but she worried her body couldn't hold on much longer. Every night, she prayed that she wouldn't become seriously ill. She needed to be healthy to work for her family. However, she could feel herself breaking down. She had already developed a foreboding cough that wouldn't go away.

Of course, there was also what happened in the waiting room. In her rare moments of free time, she worked on a letter she was writing to Elijah. They had a lot to discuss. She had written many versions, but most of them ended up in the trash. She just couldn't find a good way to say what she felt.

She also needed to talk to Chris. He had effectively disappeared. Anna tried to make time to see him, but their schedules never seemed to be compatible. The few times she had seen him were at the office, and he always left in a hurry. Working in what seemed like despair and hopelessness, she really wished he were there to offer reassurance. Brittany had angrily called him a "fair-weather lover."

When Anna suggested he simply didn't have time, Brittany waved it off. "No, Anna. That's the oldest, flimsiest excuse boys will give you. The truth is that they will make time if they want to give you time."

This only served to further depress Anna.

—-

Anna got out of the car and waved goodbye to Kelly, who had dropped her off. Autumn seemed to come early in this city. Although it was still warm during the day, she could already see golden brown leaves skating across the sidewalks as the wind blew them through the city. The cool wind exacerbated her cough, so she walked quickly towards the condominium's front door. She only had an hour to shower and change before her shift at the diner. As she walked through the glass doors into the lobby, she saw a familiar face. Chris stood by the back wall, near the mailboxes.

He took a few steps towards her. "Anna, we need to talk."

"Hm. No. You're probably busy. I wouldn't want to keep you." She turned to walk towards the elevators.

He blocked her path and she tried to go around him. He moved again. This continued for a few moments. "Anna, I'm leaving," he finally said.

She stopped. "What?"

"To Singapore. Next week."

When Anna didn't respond, he continued "I found a clinic there that would let me work before I turn eighteen. They like the research I've done about addiction treatments and want to be a part of it."

"Good for you. Is that all you came here to do? To boast?" She headed towards the elevators again.

"Well, no. I actually came to give you this." She stopped and turned around. He took a thin envelope out of his peacoat and handed it to her.

"What is this?" she asked, as she opened it. It was a check for the remainder of her hospital debt.

"It's from Brittany too," he said hurriedly as she tried to angrily shove it back into his hands.

"What?"

"Well, actually it's from the bank. We had to work together to get a loan. It's in our name, so you can pay her back over time. This way, you don't have to work yourself to death."

Anna looked at him. "Brittany says you're a fair-weather lover."

Chris smiled thinly. "I know. She called to chew me out multiple times. She really cares for you."

Anna took out the check and stared at it. "Why did someone like you need to get a loan anyway?"

He looked away. "Well, the truth is..." He paused to chuckle. "The truth is I'm kind of broke at the moment. My family really didn't approve of my move to Singapore and have threatened to cut me off. They want me here to run their businesses. My father was the only one that supported my decision. It was only because of him and your cousin that we were able to get a loan at all."

Anna felt some pity for him. "That's too bad. I had no idea."

He waved it off. "Don't feel bad. I suspected this would happen and did it anyway. I just came here to drop off the cashier's check with Brittany, but she said I should give it to you personally because I owe you an apology. I really am sorry, Anna. I genuinely have been busy preparing for Singapore, but I should have been there for you."

Anna looked down at her shoes. "I'm sorry you had to hear what Elijah said. He didn't know who you were." She looked up at him and took a breath. "About that..."

He closed the gap between them and grabbed her gently by the shoulders. "You don't have to explain it. A few moments after that Amish boy spontaneously confessed his love to you, I knew how you felt. I've seen how you look at me, and I've seen how you look at him. There's no comparison."

He looked away as he continued. "I will confess that I was a little disappointed at first, but I recognized the passion and fever in his voice as he talked about you. He had hope for a life with you. Everyone needs hope."

Anna didn't say anything, but her smile told Chris everything he needed. He took a step back and returned it. "Of course, I won't forget our time together. I'll always be here if you need a friend. That is, if you want to stay in touch?"

Anna's smile widened. "Yes, I would."

—-

It was surprising to Anna how quickly life could change. With her family's financial troubles temporarily relieved, Anna didn't need to work her second job. This allowed her body to finally get enough rest again, and her cough began to clear. She still worked hard, of course. She created a payment plan for repaying Brittany and followed it. Additionally, she had received news that her father was walking again and was expected to make a full recovery. Anna felt as if the sun had risen in her life after a long, cold night.

She also had time to finalize a letter to Elijah. She sat down and wrote from her heart. After she was done, she read what she had written:

*Dearest Elijah,*

*I was delighted to hear the news about Dad's progress. Please continue to watch over him. I know he'll be itching to get back to work, but he must take it easy.*

*I am sorry it has taken me so long to write to you. I could blame it on being busy, but truthfully... I guess I just wasn't sure how to say how I felt. I've had that problem with you since we were kids, and I guess you know how I feel. Sometimes we're still looking for the words to say...*

*Why didn't you tell me sooner, Eli? Of course I feel the same way. I never dared hope that you shared my thoughts. I suppose I feared that if I told you first, that hope might be gone. I know now that hope is never truly gone. It stays with us, and if we dare to embrace it, it shines a light on the path God meant for us to walk.*

*I must say that we will need to work on your conversational timing, though. What a moment you chose to say those things!*

*I'll need to stay in the city a while longer to work, but after that I am coming home. I'm coming home, Elijah. I have loved Chicago and I love Brittany, but this experience has only helped me realize where I need to be. I look forward to seeing you again.*

*Forever yours,*

*Anna.*

She smiled and folded the letter into an envelope. As she walked down to the mailroom, she thought about her mother, father, and siblings. She thought about living a life with Elijah and raising a family of their own. She laughed as she thought about what her friends would say about that. There was no doubt in her mind that was her home. She would be there soon.

# AMISH STRONG

94

# MARISA MEYER

## Chapter 1

Spring had awakened in the small Amish town, Mount Joy, birds were singing their spring interlude and blossoms covered the trees like frosting on a cake and the slight breeze carried its flowery sent through the village. But in the Fisher's home, it was the complete opposite. Rose Beiler's cousin Claire had gone into labour in the early hours of the morning and complications had set in. Somehow they had missed the fact she was pregnant with twins. One miracle baby had already been born and Rose was standing with the bundle in her arms while she looked on as the midwife tried her utmost to deliver the second one. Claire was in tremendous pain and agony and she had no more strength left to push.

"We need to get the Englisch doctor," Gretchen, the midwife said. Her voice desperate as she rubbed Claire's back where she lay on her side.

"And what would he do?" Rose's father muttered, standing with his straw hat in his hand.

Abraham Beiler had promised his sister on her death bed that he would protect Claire as if she was his own daughter, and with David, Claire's husband, having gone out of town, this was exactly what he was doing.

"The baby is not coming down, and it's in distress. He could do more than I can."

Rose watched her father tentatively. He was still very much old school, hated anything that represented the modern world and society. She could understand how he felt about cellular phones opening doors for evil to enter, but this was a matter of life and death. She adjusted the little baby's blanket and handed the child to the midwife.

"Daed, we cannot delay, if we don't call the Englisch doctor, Claire and the baby will die," she pleaded with her father. Her father studied her and a deep frown furrowed between his brows, the gentle touch of her hand on his arm brought his eyes to hers, "Please, we cannot lose Claire," she breathed.

"Fine!" he said frustrated, but his eyes were filled with concern.

Abraham was a muscular and tall man, people called him the Giant in jest because of his size, and although he may often come across as an intimidating individual, he had a soft heart. She knew that if he lost Claire because of his own stubbornness, he would never forgive himself, but sometimes he needed convincing.

Rose turned to her fiancé, Kemp, and nodded, "Go and hurry, Claire needs medical help urgently."

Kemp had been Rose's pillar of strength and from the age of sixteen it was a given that they would someday marry. It's been almost three years since he first made his intentions known and although their courtship had lasted a lot longer than most, she felt at ease and unburdened. She loved Kemp; he was a kind, generous and handsome man. Never had a harsh word to say and hardly ever got into any confrontations. Kemp also never said no whenever someone needed a helping hand. He was almost too good to be true.

Rose moved in next to her cousin and took her hand, "Hang in there, Kemp has gone to get the Englisch doctor, he will come and help."

Claire was incoherent and mumbled inaudibly, Rose sighed softly and said a silent prayer, then took a damp cloth to dab her cousin's feverish skin. Somewhere in the room the small cries of a newborn baby gave everyone a sparkle of hope. The midwife did everything possible to keep Claire comfortable while they waited for the doctor, but it felt as if time was in a suspended state.

An hour later, which felt like forever, Kemp burst into the kitchen and on his heels was the Englisch doctor, but it wasn't the doctor anyone expected.

"Where is Doctor Westbrook?" Abraham asked and looked out the door, half expecting him to come sauntering up the path.

"Good morning sir, I'm Dr Williams; unfortunately Dr Westbrook is at a conference in France..."

Abraham interrupted, "But you're so young."

Rose heard the commotion from the room and quickly got up to come and investigate and prevent Claire from getting too stressed.

She too was quite surprised when she got to the kitchen to find a strapping young man with a medical bag in his hand. Unlike Dr Westbrook who always arrived wearing his white coat, Dr Williams was dressed very casually, and she had to force herself to turn her attention back to the pressing matter.

"Daed, just let the doctor get on with it," Claire said and stood aside.

Dr Williams smiled confidently, "I can assure you Mr Beiler, I'm more than capable of assisting. Kemp mentioned that Claire is in labour?"

"Yah-yah, she is," Said Claire, wringing her hands nervously, "We did not know she was expecting twins. The midwife is with her, but she is not knowledgeable enough to help her."

Dr Williams nodded and skirted past Rose's father and nodded courteously at her. She glanced back at Kemp and Abraham. The concern etched on their faces matched hers. Two years ago they had buried her aunt, Claire's mother after she passed away due to pneumonia, and she knew that her father could not cope with another death in the family. *Be positive Rose*, she told herself before disappearing into the room and closing the door behind her. The less her father got to see, the better and until Claire was out of danger and the second infant was born, she would stay by her cousin's side. She just wishes David was here to support his wife.

David and Claire got married last fall, and although they looked like a happy couple on the outside, everything wasn't as peachy behind closed doors. When they first met, it wasn't a case of falling in love, it was an arranged betrothal, one Rose was opposed against, but everyone insisted that Claire marry before she turned thirty. Her mother had been overly concerned that she would end up becoming a spinster. When the bow finally broke and Claire agreed, she was introduced to David. He was from a neighbouring Amish community, only two days away by carriage. A few months after their marriage however, David kept making excuses to go back home, where he would stay for days at a time. No one else knew this, but Claire had told her that she suspected that David had another flame burning elsewhere, but it was not her place to make such accusations. Especially since David was the Bishop's son, so instead, Claire decided to simply turn a blind eye and hope it will all blow over one day.

Rose was convinced that all the stress and anxiety Claire had to deal with was the cause for her current predicament, and deep down she hated David for being so selfish. In the last few hours she had to repent more than once for feeling so angry towards him. Naturally, knowing how hard it had been for Claire to cope, she couldn't help but be nervous about her own engagement to Kemp. Especially since Kemp and David were friends. There was always that nagging voice in the back of her mind, asking her if he was really the right man for her and if she too, would one day become a lifeless bag of bones, living each day with no purpose.

*No! She couldn't entertain these negative thoughts, Kemp was nothing like David* she scolded herself and shook her head. Right now there were more important things at stake.

"When was the other baby born?" the doctor asked.

"About two hours ago," she said nervously.

"Did she have any difficulties with the birth?"

"I don't know Doctor, she gave birth, and it's not the easiest thing to do as is. What is wrong with her?"

He looked up at her and hooked his stethoscope in his ears and placed the end piece on Claire's abdomen; he listened tentatively and moved it around slowly. She couldn't help but notice the colour of his eyes. He had two different colour eyes, one hazel and one with a slight tinge of blue, which she found rather unusual. Again she had to remind herself to focus.

"Without a Caesarean section, the baby will not make it," he said and came around to look under the blanket.

"Is it that serious?" Rose asked, biting her lip.

"I'm afraid so, she's unconscious and in no position to give natural birth right now."

"Is she going to have to go to hospital?" Claire asked worriedly.

"There's no time," he said and moved around to his medical bag, "We will have to do it here."

"What!?" she cried out.

Rose's stomach bottomed out and her hand flew to her mouth, but his words were barely cold when her father stormed into the room demanding to know what was going on.

Rose calmed him down and get Kemp to take him outside while she stayed behind to assist. Everything had happened so fast, and a few minutes later, Claire's second baby was born healthy.

## Chapter 2

Grant had known that Dr Westbrook had a special group of patients he did house calls to occasionally but what he didn't expect was for them to be Amish. When the guy on the carriage pulled up in front of the medical practice, he was rather intrigued, until he discovered why he had come.

What he knew of the Amish was what he had seen on TV and online, so when he arrived there he had no idea what he was in for. But he was pleasantly surprised. Other than Mr Beiler who was a little sceptic the others were rather pleasant. Kemp was a quiet individual, he only said what was needed and didn't bother to hold much conversation. The mid-wife clearly knew what she was doing; otherwise the other baby would have gone through the same trouble. And as for the girl, whose name he learned was Rose, she was a lot more verbal than the rest. She looked like the type who could take charge if the walls came tumbling down and throughout the procedure, she remained calm and collected, following his instructions to the T.

Both babies were healthy enough, not in need of medical attention. But Claire would need a few weeks to recover, which meant he would have make daily trips to Mount Joy to check on her. At least next time around he would drive here in his own car, which would probably take 10 minutes instead of an hour.

"Dr Williams," Rose said as he headed to the door.

"Yes Rose?"

"I just wanted to thank you for saving Claire and the baby today."

"You can call me Grant," he said and smiled, "It's what I'm there for."

"I know, but thank you anyway... Grant," she smiled appreciatively.

He nodded just as Kemp pushed past him to go outside so he stepped out of the man's way, and reached out to touch Rose's shoulder, "I'll be back tomorrow to check on them."

Rose flinched, and he immediately knew he had overstepped some sort of boundary. He really needed to brush up on Amish culture and understand the do's and do not's.

## Chapter 2

The next day arrived with much promise and anticipation, Grant convinced himself that it was the mystery of this small Amish village that attracted him. It had nothing to do with the blue eyed woman in the plain purple dress and white apron, whose blonde hair was neatly tucked under her bonnet. For a moment while they worked to save the baby and Claire, he had wondered what she would look like with her hair loose.

As he drove into the small town, he was surprised to see far less people around than first expected. Compared to the day before, the town was almost half deserted and it was already past ten in the morning. Surely they would all be up and busy doing what Amish people do, by now. He pulled to a stop in front of the Beiler home and got out of his car. Even the house was quiet, and the curtains were still drawn. He contemplated waiting but as he turned to get back into his car, the front door opened.

"Dr Williams, I'm so sorry, I was busy helping Claire feed the babies."

His heart rate increased a fraction at the site of her and her half smile that caused the dimples in her cheeks to appear like wishing wells.

"Is it a convenient time or should I come back," he said. He had to remain professional. He was a doctor or heaven's sake.

"It's perfectly fine," said Rose and opened the door wider, "She's been resting, but the babies have been very restless."

Grant did whatever necessary to keep his mind focused on Claire and the babies, but with Rose hovering around like a mother hen protecting her chicks, he found it extra trying to concentrate.

"So how are you feeling Claire?" he asked, diverting his attention fully to his patient.

Claire flinched as she pushed herself up a little, "I'm fine, I'm so sorry you had to go through all the trouble to come out here."

"Oh don't apologize, it's what I do for a living, I'm just glad we saved both you and the baby. So have you named them yet?"

Claire shook her head and lowered her eyes, "No, I have to wait for my husband to return."

Rose snorted behind him, "David doesn't deserve you Claire."

"Rose! Don't talk like that." Claire looked at him, "David is a busy man, he will be here by the end of the week."

Grant noted immediately that Rose clearly did not like this David fellow, but again, it was not his place. He did however feel sorry for Claire having to have gone through this all on her own.

"And you Rose?" he asked casually not wanting to sound too fishy.

"What about me?"

"Do you have any children or a husband?"

There was a moment of silence and he looked up at her. She stood with her lips pursed and a slight frown etched on her forehead. Did he overstep again? He wondered.

"She's not married," Claire piped up.

"Claire!" Rosa reprimanded.

"What, it's the truth, you and Kemp have been courting, but nothing ever comes of it," Claire muttered and then reached to touch Grant's hand, "I think she's too afraid."

"What utter nonsense! I'm not afraid; I just don't see why I should rush anything."

Grant chuckled but didn't interject.

"What about you Doctor, are you married?"

"Oh for heaven's sake Clair, do you have to be so quizzical!" Rose reprimanded.

Grant smiled and shook his head, "I was married, but my wife is no longer alive, it's been almost four years."

"Oh goodness, I'm so sorry for your loss," Claire said with genuine sympathy.

Rose bit her lip and held her hand over her chest. The poor man must still grieve the loss of his wife and Claire is non-the-wiser.

### Chapter 3

Rose was shocked that Claire would announce her status so carelessly, and of all things holy, what gave Dr Williams the right to ask such personal questions. She had stormed out of the room and stood waiting in the living room for him to finish what he came to do while pacing impatiently. What was it about this man? Since the day he walked into this house, there was this strange feeling of longing that suddenly rose up within her soul. It was as if she was missing something in her life, but she couldn't quite put her finger on it. Maybe it was seeing Claire in such peril that made her realize just how short life was, or maybe it was the miracle of birth. She was already nearing thirty and soon her father would pressurise her into marriage, and she was still not sure if it was what she wanted, and the arrival of the Englisch doctor didn't help her either.

She was just a little girl when she had found a little fox trapped in one of the fences that bordered Mount Joy. Her first instinct was to free the poor animal, which she did and since then she always wanted to help animals. She had discovered much later, that in order to be a Veterinarian, she would need to study, but that was against God's will. Or so her father said. *A woman's place is in the kitchen, caring for her husband and children,* her father had said countless times. But while she was still unmarried, she had the freedom to tend to the horses when the men were not around. A lot of the girls laughed at her and told her she was foolish, but she never let that get her down.

She twisted the string of her bonnet around her finger as she glanced out of the window and sighed. What if she was being foolish? Maybe it was time for her to settle down and start a family of her own.

"Rose?"

Grant's voice broke into her train of thought and she turned around.

"Claire is doing as well as expected, but I will have to come back again to make sure the incision does not become septic."

Rose nodded and walked to the door, her heart racing for no reason, "I will keep an eye on her too."

Grant walked to the door but before he exited the house, he stopped and faced her, "I didn't mean to pry into your life," he whispered.

She wanted to respond to that, but her brain and her lips were suddenly disconnected. She opened her mouth to speak but nothing came out. And then unexpectedly, Grant leaned forward and pressed his lips against hers. Rose froze instantly, her arms like steel against her sides but her insides were wreaking havoc. Her heart fluttered wildly in her chest and her stomach had filled with a kaleidoscope of butterflies, all flapping their colourful wings at once.

When Grant raised his head, and the moment had passed, she slowly opened her eyes and looked into his deep soulful eyes.

"I-I'm sorry, I shouldn't have done that," he said immediately. He raised his hand as if to touch her cheek but withdrew it as if the contact would burn his fingers.

Realization swept over Rose followed by an immense feeling of guilt. She had just allowed an Englisch man to kiss her, and that while she was promised to another. Without a word she almost shoved him out the door and slammed the door shut. How could she have allowed herself to be so foolish! She had committed an adulterous sin and for that she knew she was going to be punished. But even then she could still feel the warmth of his lips on hers, and it felt so right, and so natural.

The sound of his car drifted further and further away, and only once she could no longer hear it, did she peek out of the window. Thankfully there were very few people in town this morning since they had all gone to a barn raising. She was horrified at the thought of what would happen had anyone witnessed what had just happened. She brought her trembling fingers to her lips and she let out a sigh.

"Rose!" Claire called from the room.

Rose took a deep steadying breath, fixed her bonnet and raised her chin. No one needed to know what happened, and when the doctor comes again, she would make sure she was not around. After all, she never returned the kiss.

"Do you need anything?" she asked her cousin.

"Dr Williams is a great man," she said and Rose swallowed.

"He is handy to have around," she mumbled.

"He likes you."

Rose's eyes grew as wide as saucers and she regarded her cousin, "He's Englisch, just because he asked me about my status, doesn't mean he likes me," she muttered.

"I saw the way he looked at you."

"He probably looks at every woman like that."

"Not the way he looked at you, he was taken by you."

Rose threw her hands up and shook her head, "Why are we having this conversation? Even if he liked me, you know very well that it's futile, he's not Amish. Besides, I'm happily engaged to a wonderful man, thank you very much."

Claire reached for Rose's hand and squeezed it, "Don't make the same mistakes I made, just look where that has gotten me."

Rose bent down and brushed a stray strand of hair from her cousin's face, "It's gotten you two beautiful children, and maybe, just maybe by God's grace, this is the exact thing David needs to realize what an amazing wife he has."

Claire's eyes shot full of tears and she shook her head, "No, that will never change. Maybe if we had met without the intervention of the bishop and we let things advance naturally, there would have been hope, but David does not love me. He tolerates the notion of marriage and respects the faith."

"Oh Claire," Rose said and carefully hugged her cousin, "God works in mysterious ways, he would not have put you two together was it not His will."

Claire didn't reply, simply sniffed and then plastered a brave smile on her face, "At least you and Kemp got to know each other."

"Exactly, so I'm very happy with my engagement and there's no reason for my eyes to wander to a certain doctor simply because he's handsome."

Claire laughed wholeheartedly, "So you do think he's handsome!"

"There's no denying that!"

The two women spent the rest of the morning talking about life, Rose helped Claire to feed the twins and she bathed and dressed them and saw to nappy changes. It kept her mind busy to say the least, and for the time being she forced herself not to pay a single thought of Dr Williams.


## Chapter 4

It was a lovely spring morning, and like every other morning so far, Grant was getting ready to head out to Mount Joy to see to his patient. He was about to leave when his receptionist announced that he had a visitor.

"Send him in," he said and put down the receiver.

It was Kemp who entered the rooms and although Grant was poised and calm, his insides were in a knot.

"Kemp, what brings you to town?" he asked casually.

Kemp took his hat off and clutched it in front of him, "Dr Williams, I'm sorry to barge in like this, but I was wondering if I may have a word with you?"

Uh-oh, Grant thought as he gestured for Kemp to take a seat. First thing that crossed his mind was the kiss, what if Kemp had seen it?

"So what can I do for you?" he asked curiously.

Kemp cleared his throat and sat down, "You know about the Amish yah?"

Grant nodded not sure where this was going, "A little, but not much, why?"

"Well, in the Amish, men may not study, if they do, they have to leave the community, which means they will be shunned."

Confused, Grant leaned forward on his elbows and regarded the man in front of him, "So if you want to further your education you are not allowed to?"

He nodded his head and looked down, "The thing is, I want to do what you do, I want to be a doctor and as long as I am at Mount Joy, I can't realize my dream."

Grant studied the man and he could understand exactly how conflicted he must be, "So if you decide to study, you cannot go back to Mount Joy?"

Kemp shook his head, "Yah, I can go back, but I will be like you, Englisch, I won't be able to partake in certain things, and I won't be able to marry Rose. But you see, Rose and I..."

The rest of the conversation was muted by Grant's own thoughts at realizing that Kemp was Rose' fiancé and just yesterday, he had so boldly overstepped his welcome by kissing her.

"... she will understand," Kemp said and sat back.

Grant hadn't heard a single word he was saying and shifted awkwardly in his chair.

"How do you think she would feel?" he shot in the dark.

"Rose is a strong woman, I care for her greatly but she will not stand in my way if I wish to become a doctor."

This was just too overwhelming, he thought. If Kemp was considering leaving behind everything he knew that meant he would leave Rose behind too. There was a flutter of excitement in his insides and he sat steeping his fingers together.

"I think you need to speak to Rose and tell her exactly how you feel."

Kemp nodded and then stood up, "That is what I intend to do."

Later that same day, Grant had visited Claire, but Rose was nowhere to be seen. Worried that Kemp may have spoken to her, to tell her about his plans and how she would take it, he had very nonchalantly asked Clair where she was. She was also not sure where her cousin was, but told him to wait around if he wanted to see her. He didn't, it was far too awkward, not knowing head or tail how Rose felt. He too, had some conflict, after his wife Angelique died of leukaemia he vowed never to marry again. He had loved his wife almost more than life itself and what was the hardest part of all was the fact that despite his qualifications as a medical doctor, he could do nothing about the disease that claimed his wife's life. So naturally, these feelings that started out of nowhere for a woman he hardly knew was just as much a surprise as the fact that he was falling for an Amish woman.

Over the next week or two, Grant made regular trips to the town and slowly got to know more and more of the community, occasionally he saw Rose, and although he yearned to talk to her, he couldn't bring himself to do so. She was like that breath of fresh air, a city boy needed, to get a new lease on life, but she was indefinitely out of his reach.

Kemp was also still around, and it didn't look like he had made any effort to talk to Rose about his feelings towards studying further, which led him to believe that Kemp was going to simply stay put and submit to the laws of his kin.

## Chapter 5

A month had passed, and Grant was still a regular visitor to Mount Joy, the resident doctor, the community dubbed him. But every day it had become harder and harder for Rose to cope. Her father was pressing her to decide and marry Kemp. But every time she laid eyes on Grant, she knew beyond the shadow of a doubt that she couldn't marry Kemp, not while her heart was torn in two.

It was one morning when she went to collect eggs from the chicken coop that she stole some time for herself. She needed God to guide her and help her make the right choices. She needed Him to rid her of these feelings of desire and guilt. She placed the egg basket on one of the crates and knelt down.

"Almighty God and Heavenly Father, you who know everyone's heart and failings, and who know the secrets we keep hidden, I ask you to help and comfort, and I beg you for guidance during this time. Forgive me my sins, which I have committed against you in word or deed, knowingly or unknowingly. I pray this in Your Holy name. Amen."

She had just gotten up off her knees when she heard a noise outside the coop and she went to investigate, it was Kemp and David, who had eventually returned to help Claire with the children. Afraid that they would notice her, she stayed hidden behind the wooden wall.

"I want to leave this place," she heard Kemp say.

"And go where?" asked David.

"I spoke to the Englisch doctor, I told him that I wanted to study further and also become a doctor."

Rose couldn't believe her ears, with her hand cupped over her mouth to quieten her breaths; she listened tentatively as Kemp told David that he was not ready to settle down. David warned him of the consequences of his actions too, but Kemp already had his heart set on leaving the Amish community, not so much the faith, but just to explore the world and find a bigger purpose.

Her heart ached in her chest, because like him, she always wanted to be a woman of purpose, not a simple girl working in the kitchen and seeing to a man's every need. Perhaps, this was the sign God had sent her, she thought quietly and waited for the two men to leave again. But even if this was a sign that she was not to be married now, what good would that do? She could still not consider the Englisch doctor, it was and absurd notion to say the least, and her father would have a cadenza. She was undoubtedly still stuck between a rock and a hard place, but at least it was a step closer to freedom. As soon as the two men left, she hurried to collect all the eggs, but as she stepped out of the chicken coop, the very object of her desire came walking across the field towards her. She stopped in her tracks, and even considered throwing the eggs at him to keep him away from her, but that would be silly.

"Rose, Claire told me I could find you here," he called with that heart stopping smile tugging at the corners of his lips.

"I was collecting eggs, is Claire all right?" she asked curiously.

"She's fine," he said as he stopped in front of her, "I wanted to apologise to you."

"What for?" *Apologise for the kiss or for falling into my life so unexpectedly, or for causing me to doubt my place in the Amish faith?* Her thoughts rallied.

"The kiss, I was completely out of line, and I wanted to apologise for my behaviour," he said as he crossed his arms over his chest, "I swear to you that I haven't told a single soul and I would never disgrace you."

She was surprised by his actions, but more so, she questioned them. Was he apologizing because he no longer desired her, or because he came to his senses and realized that there could be nothing between them?

"I forgive you," she simply said and gathered her skirt before sweeping past him like a gentle breeze.

"Rose..." he said, and she stopped.

"I-I don't regret it, and if I had another chance, I would do it again. You are a beautiful woman."

She felt her cheeks heat up, and she lowered her gaze, avoiding eye contact was the only thing that would keep her from dropping the eggs and running into his arms to just have one more kiss. She didn't respond to his admission though, instead, she turned and headed back towards the house, but all the while she could feel his eyes on her.


At dinner, Rose, Claire, David and Abraham sat quietly at the table; there was an eerie silence in the room.

"Is everything okay uncle?" Claire asked curiously.

"All is well," Abraham said as he poked around his plate.

Claire gave a shrug and continued eating, but Rose couldn't ignore the dreadful feeling of hopelessness that filled her insides.

"Kemp is leaving Mount Joy," Abraham said after a while, and both Claire and Rose gasped, and although Rose already knew, the finality of it came as a shock.

"He's leaving?" Claire uttered.

"Yah," David said, "He wants to study further."

Her father nodded and reached for Rose's hand, "You will find another suitor my child, if this is God's will then so be it, do not let it trouble you."

"But why didn't he tell me in person?" she asked, feigning disappointment.

"He couldn't bear hurting you, he left earlier today, but he told me to tell you that he'll always care for you," said David and dug into the potatoes.

"But we were going to marry!" Rose objected, placing her knife and fork down on the table.

"Only if God willed it," Abraham said and then continued with his meal, "The Lord, clearly has other plans for you."

Rose glanced towards Claire whose mouth was still gaping, and instead of being heartbroken she smiled at Claire, who raised an amused brow.

"I suppose it's for the best then," Claire breathed and reached for Rose's hand, "You'll find a wonderful husband yet."

Rose smiled and thanked God silently for hearing a part of her prayer at least. It had brought another season of freedom, which meant she could come and go as she pleased without the noose of marriage; to a man she cared for but didn't truly love, hanging around her neck.

As Claire got up to clear the dishes, Abraham cleared his throat, "Oh and another thing, the Englisch doctor decided to embrace the

Amish faith, and the Bishop agreed that he can continue his practice here and serve the community."

Claire dropped a plate, and it shattered on the floor and Rose nearly leaped off of her chair with excitement, but she stayed calm and collected.

"Well that's just brilliant! We could use the skill of a qualified doctor around here," Claire exclaimed as she started cleaning up her mess.

Abraham nodded, "Indeed, after what you had to endure, it didn't take much to convince the elders."

"Isn't that wonderful Rose?" Claire exclaimed but Rose simply nodded and smiled awkwardly.

In the back of the house, the wail of the twins echoed and David and Claire rushed to attend to the hungry infants.

## Chapter 6

Grant stood on the porch outside of his new home in Mount Joy; he had made a brave move to adopt the Amish faith. Not only because he secretly hoped to win the hand of Rose Beiler, but because something deep down evoked a feeling a desire to have a more substantial connection with God. The realisation that he had lost his faith came as unexpectedly as his growing feelings for Rose. All his life he had worked towards saving lives, treating illnesses and being the prophet of doom for telling families that their loved ones had passed away. And when his wife died, he somehow blamed God. It was at that time that he realized just how insignificant life really was. In the end all the knowledge he had gained and practiced could save some lives, but it could never save souls. Raised in a Christian home, he had the foundation of faith, but never really lived it. But ever since visiting this community, and as days turned into weeks and he got to spend more time with these people, he started to slowly realise that he needed to choose for the sake of his soul.

His first day as an Amish community member, had come to an end and although he was yet to be baptised, the folk were treating him like one of their own and he couldn't have asked for anything better. He was about to turn in for the evening when Rose came walking up the small path to his house and his heart thrummed in his chest.

"Good evening Rose," he said and smiled.

"Evening to you Grant, I just came to bring you some dinner. It was Claire's idea."

Grant chuckled and took the dish from Rose, "Well, your cousin clearly knows when a man needs to be fed."

Rose laughed softly and tucked a strand of hair behind her ear, "Indeed she does, anyway, may the Lord bless you."

She turned to leave, but Grant stopped her, "Do you want to have dinner with me?" he asked.

Rose laughed and shook her head, "I don't think that would be appropriate," she said but then turned and looked at him, "Maybe once you're baptised, you can offer me a ride in your buggy to a sing gathering, or to one of the church services."

Grant studied her and smirked, "Are you playing hard to get?"

"I'm playing by the rules," she said and smiled.

Grant held back the urge to pull her into his arms and silently thanked God that he had a dish in his hands, "I think I need to get my hands on the rule book and familiarise myself with these customs."

Rose laughed and swept down and plucked a small Daisy from the flower pot on the porch, "That would be wise notion doctor," she whispered and smiled before laying the daisy on top of the dish he held in his hands.

"Wise indeed, so do you promise to let me take you to the church service once I have been baptised?" he asked teasingly.

"Only if you promise to behave," she joked.

"I swear on my life," he chuckled.

~*~

A few months later, Rose stood outside the house, with Claire peeking through the window ever two minutes. Her heart was beating out of control as she waited for Grant to arrive. He had finally been baptised and although it was almost impossible to stay away from him, she managed to do so by the grace of God and hours of praying and fasting.

When Grant finally arrived, and he got out of the buggy, he grinned and walked up the stairs to meet her.

"It's been a trying time for me," he whispered as he looked down at her.

"But worth the wait?" she teased.

Grant smiled and moved his hand from behind his back holding a single Daisy in his hand, "Would you do me the honour of allowing me to take you to church?"

From inside the house, Rose could hear Claire squeal with delight and she couldn't help but laugh.

"I would be delighted," she whispered and gently took the daisy from him and placed it in her bible.

*Genesis 2:18 The LORD God said, "It is not good for the man to be alone. I will make a helper suitable for him."*

# AMISH DEPARTURE

## DEIDRA SCOTT

Chapter One

Lizzy Swartz closed her eyes and took in a deep breath of the spring air. The scent of cut grass and freshly plowed dirt put a smile on her face. She lifted her face upward, allowing the sun to warm her skin.

There was nothing like a spring day spent working out in the garden. Just the time in God's outdoors put a song in Lizzy's heart.

Suddenly, something hard hit her in the arm. Lizzy opened her eyes to see her fifteen-year-old brother, Abe, preparing to launch another clod of dirt in her direction.

"*Ach*, Abe!" Lizzy exclaimed, "Will ya never start to grow up?"

Abe stood up straighter and gave his dirt ball a toss across the garden, "Probably not," he replied, a boyish grin spreading across his handsome face.

Lizzy couldn't help but smile back, "Well, don't just stand there – pick up a garden hoe and get to work!"

"Yes, ma'am!" Abe returned in a silly tone and anxiously grabbed one of the tools, "I wouldn't want you to decide to whack me *gut* with one."

"Where's Grandpa?" Lizzy asked as she set to work chopping out some of the weeds that were starting to grow between the rows.

"He ran out to the mailbox," Abe replied.

They worked in silence for a few minutes until Abe finally asked, "Lizzy, what do you think would have happened to us if Grandpa hadn't taken us in?"

Abe's question made Lizzy stop for a moment. My, but hadn't she asked herself that question at least a dozen times? It had been almost twelve years since their parents had been killed in a tragic buggy wreck. The Amish community had been hit by hard times already with a rough drought that killed most of the area crops and left everyone feeling the strain financially. No one had enough money to take on two extra Amish children. At one point, there had been talk of sending Lizzy and Abe to foster care...but then Grandpa had stepped in.

A widower who was already shouldering the heavy job of being bishop to the Amish community, Grandpa had taken them in as if they were his own children. Although they called him Grandpa, he was completely unrelated to Lizzy and Abe.

"I don't know, Abe," Lizzy finally said with a deep sigh, "But I certainly thank God every day for sending him our way."

Abe slowly nodded his head, "*Jah*, me too."

They both worked in silence.

Grandpa had not provided them with a fancy life full of impressive possessions, but he had done his part to give them a stable home that was rich in love. Over the years, he had worked hard to instill steady morals, a love for their Creator, and a respect for hard work in the hearts of both Lizzy and her brother.

"Have you got any plans for tonight?" Abe finally asked.

Lizzy felt her face go red with embarrassment. "*Ach*, Abe," she exclaimed, "Aren't you a nosey one! Maybe I do and maybe I don't!"

"I already know you're going out with Matt Christner!" Abe exclaimed, tossing another clod of dirt at his sister, "I saw him in town and he told me."

"Well, isn't he the big mouth!" Lizzy returned with a laugh.

While Lizzy and Matt had been friends for most of their lives, they had only recently started dating. Although their relationship was new, Lizzy had already recognized that Matt was the man she wanted to eventually marry.

Lizzy's thoughts were cut short when she heard Grandpa whistling as he walked up behind her.

"Mail's here!" He announced cheerfully as he handed Lizzy a letter from her cousin in Pennsylvania.

"Didn't I get anything?" Abe asked.

"You can open mine," Grandpa told him with a laugh, tossing a handful of envelopes in his direction, "Let me know if I got anything other than bills. I'm going out to the calf barn to check on some of the babies."

Abe flipped the mail around in his hand, sorting through it for anything exciting. Stopping at one envelope, he gave a shrug and tore it open.

"Oh, Abe," Lizzy let out a laugh as she started to read the letter from her cousin, "Sally says..."

"Wait, Lizzy!" Abe exclaimed, cutting her short. Before she could protest, he called out, "Grandpa, come back here! It's important!"

Grandpa turned and hurried back to Abe's side, anxious to see what was wrong.

"*Ach*, what's happened now?" He asked, reaching for the letter.

"It nothing bad, Grandpa!" Abe exclaimed, "Its good news! Your uncle who died left you a lot of money! A lot! Yee-haw!"

"Well, I'll be," Grandpa whispered as he scanned over the document, "It surely does look like I've inherited quite a sum of money...from an uncle I don't even remember."

As Grandpa read the letter once more, Abe gave his hat a toss in the air and grabbed his sister by the shoulders, "Lizzy...we're rich!"

Chapter Two

Until Grandpa had a chance to go see the lawyer in town, they all three agreed not to tell a soul about the letter or the possibility of the inheritance. While Abe was convinced that they truly were now wealthy, neither Lizzy nor Grandpa shared his confidence.

That night, Lizzy's boyfriend Matt arrived at their house on his buggy. Although it was hard to think of anything other than the inheritance, getting to go somewhere with Matt seemed like it might distract her from the thought of money.

As she rode along beside Matt on his buggy, Lizzy found that the idea of getting her mind on something else was entirely too far-fetched to be possible.

Suddenly, Lizzy realized that Matt had hardly spoken a word to her since he picked her up at her house.

"*Ach*, Matt," she muttered, suddenly feeling ashamed of herself, "Here we've been riding together for miles and I've hardly spoken a word this whole trip. I'm sorry. I'd better watch it or you'll be picking you out a new sweetheart!"

Turning to look at Matt, she realized that he wasn't laughing or even smiling at her comments. Instead, it seemed like a dark cloud was over his handsome face.

"You shouldn't be apologizing, Lizzy," Matt replied with a deep sigh as he turned the reigns over in his hands, "I should be the one doing that. I'm not much company tonight. Probably not the best day to be takin' ya out to eat, but I sure hated to cancel. Wouldn't want you to pick out a new beau either."

Studying her boyfriend's sad face made Lizzy feel like crying herself. She knew that her Matt had been going through a rough year. His mom had been diagnosed with cancer and, although the treatments seemed to be working, Lizzy realized the family was still dealing with a lot of stress and uncertainty.

Reaching out to pat him on the shoulder, Lizzy found herself searching for the right words to say but coming up short.

"Matt," she finally said with a sigh, "The Lord hasn't forgotten about your family – he has a plan."

Matt slowly nodded his head, but Lizzy wondered if his faith was getting shaky.

The next morning, Grandpa got up early to hitch up the buggy and drive into town to see a lawyer. Although Grandpa warned Lizzy and Abe that the letter was probably nothing more than just a fake, it was impossible not to notice the hopeful glimmer in his eyes.

Waiting for Grandpa to get home was about enough to drive Lizzy mad. The hours seemed to pass so slowly and, every time Lizzy glanced toward the driveway, her heart sank as she realized Grandpa was no where in sight.

Trying to make the time pass faster, Lizzy busied herself with chores around the house. By afternoon, Lizzy had already scrubbed all of the hardwood floors, hosed off the porch, and washed the windows.

"Still no sign of Grandpa?" Abe asked as he stepped into the kitchen, looking for an afternoon snack.

Lizzy shook her head as she lowered one of the windows, "I hope he's okay."

The barking of their dog sent both Lizzy and Abe to the front door.

"He's home!" Abe squealed, jumping like a little kid as he pushed past Lizzy and started out toward the barn where Grandpa was unhitching the horses.

Not wanting to be left out, Lizzy followed close behind her brother.

By the time they reached the barn, both Lizzy and Abe were out of breath.

"Grandpa," Abe gasped, grabbing his side with his hand, "Grandpa, what happened? What did he say?"

"Help me unhitch the horses, Abe," Grandpa replied solemnly as his leathery hands set to work taking the bits out of the animals' mouths.

Abe stepped up and started working alongside his grandfather, his mouth still going much faster than his fingers, "But Grandpa, what happened in town?"

"*Ach*, Abe, we'll talk once we're all inside."

"But we're all out here, Grandpa!"

Despite Abe's pleading, Grandpa remained firm. Watching him lead the horses to an empty stall where he poured them some fresh oats, Lizzy felt her heart sink. There was no way the letter could have been true.

Once they were finished, Grandpa sat down at the kitchen table while Lizzy hurried to set a plate of fresh cookies and a glass of milk in front of him.

"Sit down, Lizzy. Sit down, Abe." Grandpa instructed.

Abe practically jumped into his seat and Lizzy felt like she couldn't grab the chair fast enough.

"Children," Grandpa finally said with a laugh, "I don't know how to tell you this...but the letter was real and the money is now in the bank. We truly are rich!"

Chapter Three

While Grandpa wouldn't say just how much money he had inherited, Lizzy realized that it must be a lot.

Sitting around the table that night, Grandpa explained that the money was something they needed to use for good purposes.

"I know how easy it is to simply waste money," Grandpa told them as he finished off Lizzy's delicious meal of homemade sweet rolls, applesauce, fried potatoes, and pork chops, "And I don't want us to waste what we have now. Before we start spending a lot of it, I want you two to come up with some ways that we could use the money to do something *gut*...not just for ourselves, but for the entire community."

Abe lowered his head, obviously a bit disappointed at the thought of having to share with the rest of the Amish.

"Can we buy a few things for ourselves?" Abe asked with 'humph'.

"Of course," Grandpa opened up his wallet and began sorting through his bills, "I know that there are things around the house that we need. Lizzy," he motioned for her to hold out her hand, "This is for you and Abe to spend on the things that we need."

Unfolding the bills that Grandpa had placed in her hand, Lizzy gasped as she whispered, "*Ach*, Grandpa, this is one-thousand dollars!"

Grandpa nodded slowly, "I think it's time that we made some improvements around here. Let me know if you need more than that."

Staring at the money, Lizzy wondered how on earth she could ever begin to think of spending one-thousand dollars on anything.

The next morning, Lizzy discovered that spending money was much easier than she had expected. When she had her driver take her to the grocery store, she planned to only spend within her usual budget. For the last five years, Grandpa had given Lizzy the sole responsibility of shopping for their weekly groceries with a very small amount of money. Lizzy had learned how to be resourceful by making purchases in bulk, off-brand items, and using coupons.

As she entered the store that Thursday morning, it seemed harder than ever to stick to her budget. Just knowing that she had one-thousand dollars to use as she saw fit made shopping seem like an entirely different experience.

When she left the grocery, Lizzy had a cart load full of groceries she would never normally purchase. After seeing how high the bils was, Lizzy promised herself she would start using their money more wisely.

Despite Lizzy's resolution to be more careful with the money, it seemed less possible with each day that passed.

Grandpa and Abe were astonished with her expensive meals that included thick steaks, but enjoyed them so much that she wasn't scolded; in fact, Grandpa reminded her to keep buying what they needed because the money was unlimited.

Although Lizzy had always enjoyed baking, the convenience of running to the store to pick up ready-to-eat loaves of bread, pies, and cookies was almost more than she could stand.

When wash day came, Lizzy even hired a driver to take her to the local laundry mat where she was able to get them cleaned and dried in a fraction of the time it took her to do the job by hand at home.

As soon as Lizzy realized that some of their clothing needed to be patched, she chose to toss the damaged items in the trash rather than keep them. When she went to pick out new fabric, the thought of sewing sounded so time consuming, that she simply hired one of the local Amish seamstresses to do the work for her.

While her work load dwindled, Lizzy took the opportunity to enjoy time reading books and going on walks in the fields.

Lizzy wasn't the only one who enjoyed the chance to indulge in some expensive luxuries. Grandpa decided that, rather than clean out the barn by hand, he would hire someone with a bobcat to do it for him.

"We need to make some serious barn repairs, too." Grandpa told Abe and Lizzy, "I'm thinking we could just hire a team of the Amish carpenters to come fix it up for us." Pausing for a moment to think, he added, "Honestly, might be even more sensible to just build a new barn all together."

"Grandpa," Luke started slowly, "I'll be sixteen next month and the age to go to the young peoples' gatherings. Do ya suppose you could just buy me a new buggy to drive? The old one's so worn out and it sure sends me in the air when I hit a bump – I'd hate to find me a pretty girl and send her sailing off the buggy seat!"

They all laughed and Grandpa nodded, "*Jah*, I don't see how a new buggy could hurt!"

Within a few days, the entire family wondered how they had ever lived on such a tight budget in the past.

Chapter Four

Saturday night, Lizzy and Matt went out on a date to the local *Englisher* restaurant in town. Whenever they went out to eat, it was a treat, but today seemed somewhat less of a thrill. With all the money that Lizzy had been spending on fancy food to cook at home, the meal seemed rather boring.

Once they had finished eating, the waitress came by and asked, "Do you want to order some desert?"

Looking at Lizzy with a smile, Matt announced, "I guess we'll take a piece of chocolate cake with ice-cream. We're splitting it, so we'll need an extra plate."

"*Ach*, Matt, sharing is such a bother." Lizzy couldn't hide her disgust at the thought of being frugal, "Let's get one for each of us!"

"Lizzy," Matt reached out and put his hand over hers, his tone little more than a whisper, "I don't have the money..."

"Don't worry about paying for it, Matt," Lizzy announced, digging through her black purse for some money, "I'll be covering the bill tonight."

Looking up at the waitress, Matt said, "Just give us one. If we need more, I'll buy a second."

The waitress looked uncomfortably from Matt to Lizzy and then back to Matt. Taking a deep breath, she nodded her head, "I'll put in the order for one. Just flag me down if you decide to get two."

As soon as she had left them alone, Lizzy found herself rolling her eyes, "Come on, Matt! What's the matter? I said I have the money. Why can't you let me pay for it myself?"

Matt shook his head slowly, "Lizzy, you don't understand. I don't want to have a girlfriend that pays for her own food. I like saving back my money and bringing you out to eat."

Unwilling to cause a scene or risk totally running their time together, Lizzy gave a curt nod and ended the conversation.

When the waitress delivered their cake, they ate in silence. Lizzy simply could not understand why her boyfriend was so stubborn!

"I'm sorry we fought in the restaurant," Matt whispered when they had finished eat and were seated side-by-side on his buggy, "I don't want us to ever argue about anything. Will ya forgive me...and still let me bring you to the young peoples' meeting Sunday night?"

Lizzy couldn't help but smile. Staying mad at her boyfriend wasn't worth the effort. Sliding over closer to him, she took a deep breath, "I'm sorry, too. *Ach*, Matt, I never would have brought up paying for it if I knew it was going to make you upset." Leaning her head against his shoulder, she took a deep breath of the night air and wished that there was some way that he, too, could enjoy the money her family had been given.

The next morning, Lizzy, Grandpa, and Abe went to church at Joe Eicher's house. Like all Amish people, the community met every other week at one of the homes of an Amish family. Preparing for the church service was a huge event that generally involved hours of cleaning and set-up.

On the way to the Eicher's house, Lizzy noticed Grandpa eyeing various things along the road. When they went past the Amish schoolhouse, he slowed the buggy down to a crawl as he pointed out the sagging roof and needed repairs.

During they church service, Lizzy watched Grandpa stare absent-mindedly at his hands. As bishop of their Amish community, Grandpa was not in charge of preaching but rather helped the entire group stay true to their beliefs.

Once they had sung the last song and church was ready to end, Grandpa stood up and raise a hand in the air.

"Before we go out to eat this delicious meal, I have an announcement to make," Grandpa said.

At his words, women stopped gathering their children and everyone returned to their seats to listen quietly to what their leader had to say.

"As everyone here knows, I've never been a rich man," Grandpa announced, "So you can imagine my surprise this past week when I discovered that I have inherited a large sum of money."

Lizzy listened as the Amish began to whisper and buzz with excitement.

"Driving past the school house today, I noticed that it needs some serious repairs." Reaching into his billfold, Grandpa pulled out a check,

"That's why I want to call Teacher Simon forward to receive a check for twenty-thousand dollars to make the necessary repairs."

Everyone gasped and then began to clap their hands.

"*Wunderbargut*!" Someone yelled out in excitement, "The children won't have to worry about it raining in on their heads any longer!" Everyone laughed.

Giving the congregation a chance to settle down, Grandpa finally announced, "I have something else to bring up, too. I know that this is different, but I want everyone here to take some time to consider this suggestion. My whole life, I've watched the women in our community burdened with the heavy load of hosting church service at their homes. I propose that we step out and build a new church building."

Suddenly, the room went silent.

Build a church? Even to Lizzy, the idea sounded strange and terribly English! Although she saw nothing wrong with the big, impressive churches in the towns, it wasn't their way at all. The Amish were simple folks and holding church within the homes was a tradition that went back hundreds of years.

As the minutes ticked by, there was still no reply to his suggestion. Finally, Joe Eicher stepped up, uncomfortably putting his hands in his pockets and refusing to look at Grandpa, "We'll have a chance to talk about all these things later. For now, my wife invites you outside to have a picnic in our front yard."

Chapter Five

Grandpa didn't stay for the picnic; instead he suggested that they stop at the restaurant in town to buy some food. Lizzy missed the feeling of togetherness she got when she gathered with her friends and family, but certainly wasn't sad to avoid the awkward stares of the others in her community.

That night, Matt pulled his buggy into their driveway at five o'clock. Lizzy had purchased some pre-made hamburger patties in town and had just finished frying them up for her Grandpa and Abe. She would eat at the young peoples' gathering.

"You're making me hungry already," Matt playfully moaned as he leaned over her shoulder. Picking up the box the patties came in, he announced, "*Ach*, we never buy these – too expensive for us poor folks." Although his words were said as a joke, Lizzy noticed something akin to scorn in his voice.

"Who could be here?" Lizzy wondered as she noticed three buggies full of Amish men pull into their drive.

Matt gave a shrug, "Looks like some of the preachers and leaders of the community."

Although she knew it was wrong to spy, Lizzy watched the men hitch their horses to the post by the porch and then step through the front door.

"Hello, Abe," she heard the men greet her brother as they walked through the front door, "Where is your grandpa?"

Lizzy picked up the plate of hamburgers and took them to the table where Grandpa was sitting just as Abe led the group of men into the room.

"Hello there, Mose," the men greeted Grandpa, "Sorry to interrupt your meal."

"No worries," Grandpa returned, "Take chairs. What's on your minds?"

As the men sat down, Lizzy and Matt stepped back into the corner, anxious to see what would happen and hoping not to be sent out of the room.

"*Ach*, Mose," one of the men finally said, "Have you plumb lost your mind?"

"Easy now, Enos," another spoke up, "Mose, we were so thankful for your contribution to the schoolhouse, but I'm afraid that I'm with Enos in asking, what were you thinking when you brought up building a church? You know that isn't the Amish way!"

Grandpa raised an eyebrow, "Come on, men! You know there's no good reason for us not to have a church building."

"Having church within the homes sets us apart from the *Englicher* world," Sam Yoder announced, "If you pull out one of the threads of our beliefs, soon we'll completely unravel! What will keep us from soon having telephones and electricity?"

"And what would be so wrong with that?" Grandpa exclaimed suddenly. In the fifteen years that Lizzy had lived with Grandpa, she had never seen him so upset about anything. She felt almost frightened as she looked into his angry face and watched as it grew redder by the minute.

The other men's eyes grew large as they stared at him.

"Ach," Grandpa finally stormed, "You don't have to like my suggestions at all, but I'll say this...building a church would help our community, and I *am* going to do it! As the bishop of our community, I have the power and with the money, I have the ability."

If the men had looked surprised before, they were totally speechless now. Finally, Enos Bontrager solemnly announced, "I'm sorry you feel this way, Mose. It seems the money has gone to your brain. You maybe the bishop of our community, but that does not mean that you are above reproach. Take some time to consider this idea of yours. If you don't submit to the Amish ways, I'm afraid the community will be forced to go over your head and inflict the *bann*."

The *bann*. Those dreadful words went through Lizzy's mind over and over again. Although she was sitting beside Matt on his buggy, she couldn't pull her thoughts away from that horrible scene at the kitchen table.

*Ach*, if the Amish chose to *bann* Grandpa, he would be completely forced from their community. He would not longer be able to eat with them – he would be entirely shunned until he repented publicly.

"What's going on with your grandpa, Lizzy?" Matt asked after taking a deep breath, obviously nervous to bring up the uncomfortable subject, "He used to be one of the easiest-going men I ever knew...now he's just acting ornery about everything!"

Lizzy instantly felt her skin bristle. Who was Matt to call her Grandpa names?

"What's that supposed to mean?" She spoke up.

"Come on, Lizzy!" Matt exclaimed, "He's changed...and you have too! Just within a week, it's like you're both different people. I don't like who you're turning into. If things don't change, he's going to end up leaving the Amish entirely."

Lizzy was so furious, it felt like she was on fire.

"Grandpa is one of the best men I know!" She snapped, "If he wants to build a church building, then I'm completely behind him. If you have a problem with it, then maybe we should stop seeing each other. And, if the Amish are going to be so stubborn that they won't accept his gift, then maybe I don't want to be Amish anymore!"

"Lizzy..."

"Just drive," She snapped, folding her arms across her chest and scooting as far away from her boyfriend as she could.

That night, Lizzy sat in her bedroom, thinking about life as she prepared for bed. Lizzy brushed her hair out slowly and stopped to study herself in the mirror. While mirrors weren't usually found in Amish houses, Lizzy had made a secret purchase over the weekend.

Gazing at herself, she tried to gauge how pretty she was compared to the other Amish girls. But wouldn't she be prettier if she had some of that fine paint the *Englishers* wore on their faces!

Instantly, she pushed the thought away, wishing that she hadn't let it run through her mind.

With all that was going on with her grandfather, she truly wondered if they would be left in the Amish church. What Matt had repeated was what all the Amish were thinking. Grandpa was determined to go forward with his plans to build a church...and the Amish community wasn't going to stand for it. There was a good chance that they might get shunned. If that happened, she wondered what Grandpa would do. Would he turn his back on the Amish way entirely? And, if he did, would she go with him?

"Lizzy, Lizzy," she scolded herself, "What are you a thinkin'? Consider Matt!"

But, the more she considered Matt, the more clouded her thinking became. She had been so certain that he was the man she wanted to marry and spend the rest of her life beside, but the money had changed everything.

Lizzy was beginning to like the feeling that money gave her. It made her happy to know that she and her family were a step above the rest of those in their community. She was tired of the work that she had to do as an Amish woman.

If they left the Amish, she would be free to own a washing machine and a drier, a refrigerator, and even a television! Putting aside her brush, Lizzy ran her hand through her hair and took a deep breath.

She was almost scared of what tomorrow might bring.

Chapter Six

All Monday morning, Lizzy found herself looking out the window, afraid that she would see more of the church leaders coming up the drive. In some ways she was frightened, while in others she was almost hopeful.

Grandpa sat at the table, working on a design for the new church. Since the Amish community was set against having it built, he had already contacted a team of English carpenters who could do the work.

That afternoon, someone finally did come up the drive. When Lizzy saw that it was Matt, she couldn't decide if she was more relieved or disgusted.

"Lizzy," Matt took off his straw hat and twisted it between his hands when she invited him inside, "Could we go on a walk and talk?"

Preparing for a lecture, Lizzy braced herself and started across the yard beside him.

Suddenly, Lizzy was surprised when she looked up at Matt and noticed tear drops running down his cheeks. Instantly, her defenses were down and her heart filled with worry for this man she loved so much.

"What's wrong Matt?" Lizzy asked as she reached out to pat her boyfriend on the arm,

"Lizzy," Matt took a deep breath and let it out, "I don't know what to say. My *maam*'s finally going to come home, but now the hospital wants us to start paying our bills. She's got to keep taking treatments and they're expensive, too. Dad doesn't even know how he's going to do it at all. He's talking about selling the farm."

"Selling the farm!" Lizzy exclaimed, "What would you all do then?"

"*Daed*'s talking about moving back to Pennsylvania. There's nothing for us here if we have to sell everything. We can move in with my grandparents until mom's treatments are finished."

"Surely there will be some other way..."

"Lizzy, my dad already took out a gigantic mortgage on the farm. He's not going to be able to pay it back." Shrugging, Matt announced, "I don't know when we're likely to move, but I'd like the little bit of time we have left together to be good. I'm sorry about last night."

"No, I'm sorry," Lizzy whispered. Reaching out, she wrapped her arms around her boyfriend and pulled him close to her.

That night, Lizzy picked up some food at the restaurant because she didn't feel like cooking. Her heart felt so heavy whenever she thought about Matt and his family. She told Grandpa and Abe. Suddenly, they were no longer concerned about building fancy churches or fighting with the Amish. They just sat together silently, each lost in sorrow over the situation of Matt's family.

"I wish that there was something we could do," Abe muttered softly, "I've always though a lot of Matt's family."

"*Ach*," Grandpa exclaimed as he slammed his hand against the tabletop, "What on earth are we doing? I always looked down on people who had money and were selfish with it...and yet I find that I'm exactly the same way."

"Grandpa!" Abe looked at him in surprise, "How can you say that you're selfish? All you want to do with your money is good! You want to make a better life for us...and you want to help out the church and the community with buildings. How can that be wrong?"

Grandpa shook his head slowly, "In the midst of all our figuring, did we ever stop to even think to ask the Lord what He would want us to do with this money? No. Instead, we chose to plow ahead and do what we thought was best."

Everyone was silent as they looked down at their plates in deep thought.

"Tonight, this ends!" Grandpa announced, reaching out to take Abe's hand in one of his own and Lizzy's in the other, "Tonight we're turning to the Lord to find out what he wants."

The next morning, Grandpa took the money that Lizzy had left over and went to town.

"Well," Abe muttered softly as he worked alongside his sister in the garden, "I sure did enjoy being rich."

"As did I," Lizzy said with a sigh, "But I think I'll be glad to be plain Lizzy once again."

When Grandpa got home, he came out to the garden to work alongside them.

No one said a word until Abe finally ventured to ask, "Do we have anything left at all?"

Grandpa shook his head, "I paid off all of Matt's family's debts and then gave the rest as a donation to the hospital. I've already been to talk to some of the church leaders and apologized for the entire church building idea."

"How are we ever going to make it now?" Abe grumbled, kicking at a clod of dirt with the toe of his work boots.

Grandpa smiled, "I suppose the way we always have...a lot of pinching pennies and patching up clothes. In the end, we did what that Lord wanted and we did what was best for other people who needed the money much worse than us."

"I never did get my buggy," Abe said with a sigh.

"Ahh...that is true." Grandpa gave the teenager a pat on the shoulder, "How about you and I work on that old buggy together. I think if we put some time into it, we can have it good as new."

"And, when you go courting, maybe you can just tell her to hang on tight before you hit a bump in the road!" Lizzy suggested.

They all laughed, finally able to enjoy one another's company without the distraction of money.

Working together silently, they listened to the sound of the birds chirping overhead and enjoyed the cool breeze drifting through the trees.

Prologue

Lizzy smiled to herself as she sat on the homemade wooden swing on the front porch. Although it had been hard to give up the money, she had to admit that a simple life truly was the right one for her.

Looking up from a page in the book she was reading, Lizzy realized that Matt had pulled his buggy into their yard and was coming toward her.

"Hello, Matt," she announced, wishing that she and her beau had never gone through such a rough spot.

Without saying a word, Matt took a seat on the swing beside her.

"It was your grandpa, wasn't it?" Matt asked slowly as he reached out and took Lizzy's hand in his own, "He was the one who helped to cover my *maam*'s doctor bills, right?"

"Matt..." Lizzy looked down at her feet, trying to decide how much she should even start to share, "Ach, Matt, he doesn't want a bunch of people to know. He wanted to keep it a secret. The way Grandpa looks at it, the money wasn't ours to start with...it was just something that God had loaned us so that we could use it to help others. He got off track because of it...we all did, I'm afraid. I'm sorry that I was so harsh to ya, Matt. It was wrong of me. I let the love of money cloud my thinking. Grandpa reminded us that we should pray about what to do with it, and from that point on, it all just became clear."

Matt shook his head, "That's the kind of man I wish that I could be. Lizzy," he took a deep breath, "I'm no where near as great a man as your grandpa, but I'm going to try my best to be a *gut* Amish man who loves his family, helps his neighbors, and serves the Lord. Would you be willing to go through this journey with me...as my wife?"

Lizzy felt her breath catch in her throat and she wondered if she could even start to speak. After all that had happened between them, she was afraid that Matt would be ready to end their relationship completely. She opened her mouth and words wouldn't come out. Instead, all that would come were tears of joy.

"Oh no," Matt teased jokingly, "Looks like you're not very happy with my question!"

*Lizzy threw her arms around his neck and let her warm embrace give her answer. Pulling away from the man that she loved, Lizzy exclaimed, "Ah, Matt, being married to you is going to be better than all the money in the world!"*